The Fable of Flitcroft Point

A CONTROVERSIAL NOVEL THAT TURNS
NEW ZEALAND HISTORY UPSIDE-DOWN

ROBERT PHILIP BOLTON

Also by Robert Philip Bolton
Jacko. One Bloke. One Year.
The Boys and Men of Auckland's Mickey Rooney Gang
The Fine Art of Kindness
Six Murders?
To The White Gate
Underneath The Arclight
My Marian Year
The Boltons of The Little Boltons
The Tapu Garden of Eden
For Viktor. The story of Mussorgsky's 'Pictures at an Exhibition'
The Collected Short Stories (in which is combined *Nana's Special Day and other stories, The Dolphin and other stories,* and *Quickies.*)

Robert Philip Bolton was born in New Zealand in 1945. He has been writing most of his adult life. Most of his work is about New Zealand and New Zealanders. He lives in Auckland.

The Fable of Flitcroft Point

Bastion Point land returned

1 July 1988

The government announced that it had agreed to the Waitangi Tribunal's recommendation that Takaparawhā (Bastion Point) on the southern shore of Auckland's Waitematā Harbour be returned to local iwi Ngāti Whātua.

Protesters had occupied Bastion Point in early 1977 after the government revealed that expensive houses would be built on former Ngāti Whātua reserve land. The reserve had been gradually reduced in size by compulsory acquisition, leaving Ngāti Whātua ki Ōrākei tribal group holding less than 1 ha. The protesters, under the banner of the Ōrākei Māori Action Committee, refused to leave their ancestral lands and occupied Bastion Point for 506 days.

On 25 May 1978, when the government sent in a massive force of police and army personnel to evict the occupiers, 222 protesters were arrested and their temporary meeting house, buildings and gardens were demolished. The Bastion Point occupation became one of the most famous protest actions in New Zealand history.

Ten years later the Waitangi Tribunal supported Māori claims to the land, and the government accepted this finding.

From New Zealand History online: https://nzhistory.govt.nz/

1

IT WAS FOUR o'clock one cold morning in May when Fannie Flitcroft died in childbirth. Her baby was already dead; his little dull-blue, damp-haired head hung loosely between his dead mother's spread legs on the wet and bloody coarse cover of the mattress.

The midwife, frantic and desperate, was skilled and experienced, but nothing had prepared her for this. Her screams of fear and frustration brought Cyril Flitcroft, the dead woman's husband — the dead child's father — bursting into the room with his mother, Ida.

The old woman saw immediately that the usually-capable midwife was now capable of nothing. She saw what was necessary; that there was no choice. She instructed her son — the newly-widowed husband — to hold the shoulders of his dead wife while she gently drew out the dead infant until it flopped lifelessly onto the mattress, linked still to the dead mother by the thick umbilical cord.

'God bless the poor child,' said Ida Flitcroft sadly, knowing that there was now next to no chance she would be a grandmother again. Cyril was her only child and he had only the now motherless young Arthur.

What on earth, she wondered, did this awful life hold for that poor boy?

Arthur had been woken by his mother's screams, which were followed by the midwife's screams for help. Frightened, unable to sleep, he wrapped himself in a warm blanket and waited anxiously in the hall, sitting on the floor in his pyjamas, leaning against the wall.

He stood up quickly when his father and grandmother emerged from the bedroom.

'Papa?' he asked, looking weary, puzzled, and worried.

'Your mother's dead, boy,' said Cyril plainly, resting his hand on the boy's head. 'I'm sorry but...'

'And the baby?'

'The baby, too, I'm afraid.'

At that, the confirmation from his father that his worst fears had been realized, the eleven-year-old now-motherless Arthur Flitcroft slid again to the floor, rested his crossed arms on his raised knees, his forehead on his arms, and cried.

*

He didn't cry when, at the end of the next day, a Saturday, the bodies of his mother and brother, wrapped together in a loose but tied white shroud, were laid carefully at the bottom of the grave by the gravedigger, his father.

But he did cry, as did his grandmother — but not his father or grandfather — when first his father, followed by others, dropped clods of damp earth into the grave. He saw them land heavily on the shrouded bodies as his great-grandfather, Enoch, solemnly read the burial prayers from the old book he had inherited from his own father, the priest, the contents of which — rites and prayers for every Christian occasion — were more than six hundred years old.

Enoch's voice was strong enough but Arthur thought his great-grandfather looked old and frail.

'For as much as it hath pleased Almighty God of his great mercy to take unto himself the soul of our dear sister Fannie Anne Flitcroft here departed,' read Enoch, the *de facto* priest, 'we therefore commit her body to the ground. Earth to earth, ashes to ashes, dust to dust, in sure and certain hope of the resurrection to eternal life, through our Lord Jesus Christ who shall change our vile body that it may be like unto his glorious body according to the mighty working, whereby he is able to subdue all things to himself.'

Arthur wondered why his dead little brother had not been mentioned.

His mother's funeral and burial was the first time he had spent time in the village cemetery, although he had often been taken to the little church there. But now he knew he would come back often to visit his mother and brother buried, with many others of his Flitcroft ancestors, in that narrow but important and historic strip of land at the edge of Flitcroft beach.

*

When Arthur's birthday arrived — not even a month after his mother's death — his grandmother, Ida, informed him before school that he had just turned twelve years old.

It was the first time he had been told the date of his birth. Since the sicknesses had passed, long ago, the Kiwilanders had never celebrated birthdays.

It was a cold Tuesday, Arthur's birthday. Old Enoch was still in bed while Cyril and his father, Alfred — Arthur's grandfather — had gone out early to the farm's extreme south paddock to check on the young beasts there. Arthur was therefore alone in the kitchen with his grandmother. Ida had made the men's breakfast and was now sitting with Arthur in front of the warm stove.

'Everyone did what they could, you know, boy,' she said after a while of contemplation.

Arthur didn't know what to say; what to ask. But he hoped his grandmother would keep talking as his father never talked about that night

— that awful night when his mother and baby brother died — to him or anyone.

'The ambulance came,' she said. 'At last they came. But it was too late. She was already gone.'

'Why?' asked the boy with a sad and pleading look. 'Why didn't they come in time? I don't get it.'

'It's a long way from Whangārei, boy,' said Ida. 'They're not so heartless to *not* send help. But they're very important and busy and us Kiwilanders, well, we're not top of their list are we.'

It wasn't a question.

'But they might have saved her life. And the baby.'

'I'm sorry, boy,' said Ida, 'but, honestly, I'm not sure that even the best Vandier doctor from Auckland could have saved her.'

'It's just not fair,' said Arthur sadly.

'I know, boy,' said Ida. 'Life's just not fair. It is our lot, I'm afraid. The Kiwilanders' lot.'

Arthur could see that his grandmother was trying her best to take over his mothering.

'But Papa. He never...'

'Don't blame nothing on your papa,' continued Ida. 'He's sad too, you know. Perhaps he doesn't know what to say.'

Arthur shrugged.

'And him and your grandpapa must work so hard,' continued the old woman. 'He couldn't look after you on his own.'

'I know,' said Arthur sadly, resignedly.

'Perhaps if you work hard at school you'll get a better job than working on the farm like them.'

'I do work hard at school,' said Arthur.

Arthur was a keen scholar. He went daily to the village school where the teachers were all Vandiers who gave all lessons in Vandient. Indeed, none of the teachers could speak English — few Vandiers could — and so, at school, the children were forbidden to speak the language which they used at home and to each other when not at school.

Thus, Kiwilander children routinely learned to speak two languages, an achievement seemingly beyond the ability or even desire of adult Vandiers.

2

'YOUR FAMILY — NOT mine — the Flitcrofts, they were here first,' Ida told Arthur on his birthday. 'Before the village even existed, this was your family's land. This farm, here, beside the sea, for many generations, even before your Great-Grandpapa Enoch was born.'

The old woman was relating what she had been told by old Enoch. It wasn't right in every detail but it was right enough.

'First,' she said, 'early in the twenty-first century, more than a hundred-and-fifty years ago, came the mysterious sicknesses.'

She was right about that. At that time no one in Kiwiland — in the world — could understand what was happening, where the sicknesses had come from, and how they could be cured. It seemed that when one faded away another arrived and then multiplied and mutated at a rate faster than the primitive science of that distant time could match. As a result, no island or atoll, no country or continent in the world escaped their reach. Billions of people died. And in Kiwiland, no farm, village, town or city was unaffected.

Although no cure was ever found, the sicknesses eventually retreated. This took more than fifty years, however, during which time the world's population had been reduced to the one person in five who had somehow acquired immunity or had inherited it from some ancient genetic material.

As a result, with eighty per cent of its population dead, the world descended into famine and chaos.

'The Kiwilanders' population was then just one-fifth its size before the sicknesses,' said Ida. 'And we've never recovered.'

In the end there were simply not enough people left in the Kiwiland countryside with the health, energy, knowledge and experience to properly manage the vast and productive lands left to them — agricultural and horticultural — and their huge animal populations. Meanwhile, in the towns and cities, there were not enough people left to process, transport, preserve, store, and sell the food, even if enough were being produced.

Thus, despite being surrounded by an abundance of food, Kiwiland's surviving populations, urban and rural, were threatened with famine. And so the survivors — urban and rural both — came together, in places all over the country, like the Flitcroft village, where they were forced by circumstances to dismiss their petty differences and work together to survive.

The city folk — ignorant of land management, crop growing and harvesting, animal husbandry and butchery, and the hard labour that success demanded — were compelled to learn the rudiments from the those few experienced country folk who had survived. And they, the country people, forced to be unjealous of land ownership, welcomed both the company of the refugee townsfolk and the labour they provided. Town and country, therefore, came together for their mutual survival. They had no choice.

Meanwhile, though, the towns and cities of Kiwiland were left, abandoned and empty.

*

There was no Flitcroft village when four-year-old Enoch Flitcroft fled with his family from their home in Whangārei. Enoch's father had been a minister of the Church of England but, having no choice, they — the Reverend Henri Flitcroft and his wife, together with young Enoch and his two older sisters — went north-east to the remote Northland coast where Henri's brother maintained the Flitcroft family farm.

The farm was set in a fertile valley that ran gently down to a pleasant beach. It was bounded to the north by a high, rounded promontory — known for generations and still as Flitcroft Point — which stretched out to sea, providing uninterrupted and spectacular views up and down the Northland coast and far out to the Pacific Ocean.

Four other farms defined the Flitcroft's west and south boundaries but by the time the fleeing Henri Flitcroft arrived with his family the Flitcroft farm was the only one working, the others having been abandoned when their owners and their entire families had succumbed to the sicknesses and no other heirs or relatives had come forward to claim ownership. And so a village quickly arose on the vacant farmland adjacent to the Flitcrofts'.

At first the village was no more than a row of tents and ramshackle huts on the abandoned land bordering the inland boundary of the

Flitcroft farm, but it quickly grew when many other surviving Kiwilanders followed the Reverend Flitcroft, seeking company, security and, above all, food.

The young and devout priest, Henri Flitcroft — Enoch's father — was only twenty-seven when he was forced to take his family and join his brother on the Flitcroft farm. He was healthy, strong and energetic, and a methodical organizer by training and temperament. As more survivors arrived from Whangārei, joining others on the Flitcroft farm boundary, he set about imposing some order on the settlement by laying out what they called Main Street, and a few side streets and lanes, assigning plots of land, and recording the names of the settlers as "owners".

He and his brother also cut a track through the farm, from Main Street to the beach — which became known as Beach Street — to provide the village with free and easy access to the coast.

'But then,' said Ida to the attentive Arthur, 'almost straight away, according to your Great-Grandpapa Enoch, the Vandiers came.'

'But couldn't we stop them?' asked Arthur naively.

'They came in such great numbers,' said Ida. 'Your Great-Grandpapa will tell you. He remembers it well, even though he was only five years old. How they came by sea and air, with great sea-ships and air-ships and powerful weapons against which our little Kiwiland forces were powerless.'

'But didn't they try?' asked Arthur.

'Oh, they tried,' said his grandmother. 'They tried, but it was useless. There were battles. Many of our people were killed by their clever weapons.'

'I didn't know, Grandmama,' said Arthur.

'Well, you know now,' said Ida. 'And about time. They came, took over our cities and factories, paying not in their Vandier money — for which our people had no use — but in the building materials and farm machinery which were so desperately needed. And they restarted the electricity and the water and built the V-services, and so much more.'

A hundred years later Flitcroft was a small but tidy and well-established little village of industrious Kiwilanders. Most worked in Whangārei, in the Vandiers' factories, travelling there and back on the V-3 Local service. Others worked on the large Flitcroft farm, or co-operatively cultivated the once-abandoned backlands behind the town, raising animals and poultry — anything that could be turned into meat — and growing seasonal vegetables and fruits. There was also a small fishing fleet which, in fine weather, set out for two days of fishing. After keeping enough to feed themselves, the farmers, gardeners, orchardists and fishers took everything to Whangārei where it was sold in the markets.

There were some Vandier residents in the village including a few shopkeepers, the superintendent of the V-station, and the Superior of the Peace Force and his wife who was Arthur's teacher.

It was their son who was to become Arthur's fateful friend.

3

DESPITE THE CHAOS all around him then — it was 2078 when the church was built — young Henri Flitcroft was still a priest and so officiated there, in his new little church, on Sundays and holy days as well as at weddings, christenings and funerals, reading from the Book of Common Prayer and drawing inspiration from the Bible and other texts which he had brought with him from Whangārei.

Meanwhile the Vandier government, while tolerant of the Kiwilanders, despised their language, culture, traditions and religious beliefs. In particular they thought the Kiwilanders' worship of a being believed to be half-man half-god to be absurd. And they considered the Kiwilanders' ritualized eating of bread and drinking wine — symbolizing the consuming of the man-god's human flesh and blood — to represent an ancient practice of human sacrifice and cannibalism. Altogether, the government considered the Kiwilanders' religion to be no better than a collection of primitive superstitions harmful to their mental health and welfare, impeding their progress towards Vandier civilization.

As a result the government acted — in 2107 — to ban the Kiwilanders' priestly class and all priestly activity.

At that, Henri Flitcroft — then not even sixty years old — fell into wretched despair and soon died, sad and miserable. His wife had died eighteen years earlier so he was survived by his bachelor son, Enoch, and Enoch's two older married sisters. Thus Enoch became the custodian of his father's holy books and acted as an elder, reading from them at weddings and funerals.

It was he who officiated at the burial of his own grandson's wife and baby — Arthur's mother and stillborn brother — at the grave dug by Cyril in the little village churchyard to which he had such a close connection.

*

It was at the foot of that grave that Arthur stood late one fine day in the middle of November, six months after that fateful May day. A proper headstone had been installed from which Arthur, not knowing how else to acknowledge his mother, now read aloud.

FANNIE ANNE FLITCROFT

11 JUNE 2140 – 17 MAY 2176

(AGED 36 YEARS)

BELOVED WIFE OF CYRIL ERNEST FLITCROFT
AND MOTHER OF ARTHUR HENRI FLITCROFT

ORPHANED ONLY CHILD OF HAROLD AND MARY
HAZELTINE

There was no mention of the dead baby; Arthur didn't know why.

'That's your mother, isn't it?' said someone in Vandient from behind him.

It gave Arthur a start. He turned around and recognized the boy; Mot-L, a Vandier boy about his age who travelled daily to Whangārei for his education at an expensive private school.

'Yes,' said Arthur, replying hesitantly in his best Vandient.

Because he knew he had a Kiwilander accent — which the Vandiers liked to ridicule — Arthur was always embarrassed to speak Vandient with a native Vandient speaker.

'I thought so,' said Mot-L. 'I'm sorry.'

'Thank you,' said Arthur in reply. He continued in Vandient as he had no choice. 'You're Mot-L, aren't you.' It wasn't a question. 'Your mother is my teacher at school. And your father is the Peace Force Superior.'

'That's right,' said Mot-L. 'And you're Arthur Flitcroft. Your Vandient is pretty good.'

'Thank you,' said Arthur again.

'Better than my English which is actually non-existent,' said the Vandier boy with an embarrassed laugh. 'I'm sorry.'

'That's all right,' said Arthur. 'I can speak Vandient.'

'Call me Mot-L,' said the Vandier boy.

'I know,' said Arthur. 'Call me Arthur.'

'I wish I *could* speak English,' said Mot-L. 'I really do.'

'But why? I thought...' said Arthur.

'I know. It's not done. To speak English. But I'd like to learn. Really.'

Despite the boy Mot-L's relaxed friendliness, and apparent eagerness to learn English, Arthur found his presence disconcerting. He had never seen a Vandier — adult or child —in the cemetery or anywhere at all on the church grounds thinking, wrongly, that their presence there was forbidden.

'I've got to go,' he said suddenly.

He turned away then, towards the cemetery gates, anxious to escort the Vandier boy out of the cemetery and more especially away from his mother's grave.

Later, when quizzed by his grandmother, Arthur couldn't remember exactly how he and Mot-L had become such good friends. He knew it had begun following their encounter at the cemetery and that it quickly developed into a genuine friendship. They soon fell into meeting almost every day after school in the shed at the side of the Flitcroft garden in which Ida stored her gardening tools, seeds, seed trays, chemicals and fertilizers.

There, in private, away from village eyes who would judge them both, for opposite versions of the same reason, Mot-L coached Arthur in spoken Vandient by correcting his clumsy pronunciation and then, using his school textbooks, taught him how to read and expertly write the complex characters of printed Vandient.

Gradually but inevitably Mot-L began to better understand and speak English merely through being in Arthur's presence. This quick improvement encouraged him greatly until he asked Arthur if he would coach him properly to understand and speak English just as he was coaching Arthur in Vandient. He said that reading and writing English could wait; he first wanted to be fully competent in the *spoken* language; to be understood as well as to understand.

Meanwhile the two boys of matched intellect played chess, taking many days to complete each game. Arthur possessed one of his great-grandfather's ancient chess books, *Bobby Fischer Teaches Chess*. It had to be handled with special care but served to improve both their chess and language skills as well as introducing Mot-L to the English printed word.

Ida, who worked at home all day, noticed the boys' friendship and secretly hoped it would come to nothing. She knew the contempt in which poor Kiwilanders — which meant *all* Kiwilanders — were held by the Vandiers and didn't want her sensitive grandson exposed to their prejudices.

She didn't mention the matter to the men then, deciding instead to first speak to Arthur; to warn him of what might come from his friendship with a Vandier boy.

One afternoon before dinner, after Mot-L had gone, Ida insisted that Arthur sit down with her in the kitchen. Old Enoch was dozing in his bedroom, and so they were alone.

'How come you're friends with that Vandier boy?' she asked.

Arthur shrugged. 'Just a friend, Grandmama,' he said.

'But why him?' insisted Ida. 'There are plenty of Kiwilander kids in the village, but you're friends with one of the only Vandier kids. And his father's the big boss of the Peace Force.'

Arthur shrugged again as children do when they know the answer but don't want to give it; he didn't know how to easily explain his friendship with Mot-L.

'At school, boy,' continued his grandmother. 'Plenty of Kiwilander boys. Why aren't you friends with any of them? Like Doral Turpin. He lives just up the road.'

'I *am* friends with them,' insisted Arthur. 'And I see Doral every day at school. But Mot-L is my *best* friend, that's all.'

'Why?'

'Why what, Grandmama?'

'Why is he your *best* friend? What's so special about him?'

'He is teaching me proper Vandient,' said Arthur.

'But you *know* how to speak Vandient,' said Ida. 'Everyone does.'

'Yes. But he's teaching me to speak it properly, like a Vandier, without an accent. And how to read and write complicated grown-up things that aren't in schoolbooks.'

'How will you ever understand hard stuff like that?'

'I'm learning,' said Arthur indignantly.

'And what does the boy get out of it?'

'I'm teaching him English,' said Arthur.

'What?' Ida was astonished. 'I never ever heard of no Vandiers wanting to learn English.'

'Well, *he* does. And we play chess, Grandmama.'

'You mean that boy has no one to play chess with except a dumb Kiwilander kid?'

Arthur was mortified. 'I am *not* dumb,' he protested.

'*I* know you're not dumb,' said Ida quickly, immediately regretting using the word. 'But that's what *they* think, isn't it. The Vandiers. They think we're all lazy, dumb Kiwilanders.'

'Well, Mot-L's not like that.'

'Mot-L,' said Ida scornfully. 'What sort of name is that anyway?'

'It's a Vandier name,' said Arthur. 'An ordinary Vandier name. Like Arthur's an ordinary name for me.'

'Huh!' scoffed Ida again. 'And what does his big, important father think of his boy having a Kiwilander friend?'

'He doesn't know,' said Arthur.

'Oh no,' said his grandmother shaking her head slowly, almost fearfully. 'A secret. That makes it even worse, boy.'

'Why?' asked a genuinely puzzled Arthur.

'To keep the secret. The boy must be ashamed to have a Kiwilander friend. Afraid of what his father would think.'

'No he's not,' said Arthur quickly. 'It's not that at all.'

'What is it then?'

'Listen, Grandmama.' Arthur was almost pleading. 'Mot-L really wants to learn English. But he also wants me to help him at chess. To get good enough to beat his father. His father always beats him, see. We can do it with Great-Grandpapa's old chess book. The Vandiers have nothing like that book so his father doesn't know about that man from the olden days who wrote it. That's all. That's why he hasn't told him about me. He wants to surprise him when he beats him at chess.'

'It's much more than that, boy,' said Ida, shaking her head. 'And if your old Great-Grandpapa Enoch knew, well, I don't know…'

'Don't tell him, Grandmama, please. I know what he, and Papa and Grandpapa too, I know what they think of the Vandiers. Please, Grandmama.'

At which pleading the old woman nodded in agreement; but reluctantly.

4

IT WAS ON the Monday afternoon before Christmas, 2176, after what was to be his last garden-shed meeting of the year with Mot-L, that Arthur came inside to find Ida sitting at the kitchen table, her head in her hands.

By then his Vandier friend had achieved his objective of speaking English as fluently as a native speaker, without a give-away accent, and to read and write it adequately which was better than any Vandier he knew. And Arthur was now able to speak Vandient fluently, without a Kiwilander accent, and read and write it as quickly and easily as he read and wrote English.

And so, feeling pleased with himself, Arthur was surprised to see, when his grandmother looked up, that she had been crying.

'Where's your father and grandfather, boy?' she asked abruptly with a worried look.

'I don't know, Grandmama,' said Arthur. 'They must be home soon.'

He didn't know what to do; until his mother's funeral he'd never seen his grandmother crying before. What awful thing has happened now? he wondered.

'Are you all right?' he asked, puzzled.

'I'll be all right, boy,' said Ida, wiping her wet and reddened eyes with a handkerchief. 'I'll be all right but I need to talk to the men.'

It was then they heard Cyril on the porch, removing his boots. Arthur felt awkward about his grandmother's tears, embarrassed for her as much as for himself, and decided to leave her problem, whatever it was, to his father. He went to his room as his father came into the room.

'Where's your father?' Ida asked Cyril at once.

Cyril, too, could see that his mother had been crying. He didn't comment but pointed over his shoulder with his thumb. 'He's coming,' he said. 'A bit slow.'

'He's getting too old for farm work you know,' said Ida with a sniff.

'I know, but he insists on helping,' said Cyril. 'Anyway, what's the matter?'

'Wait for your father. I'll tell you both.'

'Where's the boy?' Cyril asked.

'He's gone to his room I think,' said Ida. 'A bit embarrassed I suppose. Me crying and that.'

'Was he with that Vandier boy again?'

His mother nodded.

'I don't like it,' said Cyril.

'He's all right,' said his mother. 'I think.'

'You *think*?'

'He's a nice boy,' said Ida. 'Polite. To me, anyway. And he likes Arthur and that's important.'

'Why's that important?'

'Haven't you noticed?' said Ida. She had stopped weeping and so slipped her handkerchief into the pocket of her apron.

'Noticed what?'

'Your Arthur's not like other boys, Cyril. He's clever. Don't you realize that? So he doesn't make friends easily.'

'Doesn't he?' Cyril was surprised. He didn't see Arthur often. He had left his mother to do the parenting.

'No.'

'I didn't know,' said Cyril with a shrug.

'That boy Mot-L's clever. Like Arthur.'

'Who's Mot-L?'

'The Vandier boy,' said Ida. 'His name's Mot-L.'

'Oh,' said Cyril. 'His father's the Peace Force Superior isn't he?'

Ida nodded grimly.

'That's not good,' said Cyril with a slow shake of his head.

'I know,' said Ida. 'But your boy needs a good friend. Someone clever like him. Like this Mot-L boy. He still misses his mother you know, and a good friend...'

'I s'pose I should have done more,' said Cyril somewhat sadly. 'But what with...'

'I know, son,' said Ida. 'To lose a young wife. And a baby.'

Cyril shrugged. 'And work,' he said.

'Christmas makes you think about things, you know,' said Ida.

Cyril nodded but said only: 'So you think it's all right? That Vandier boy, I mean.'

'I don't know for sure, do I,' said Ida. 'But he helps Arthur with his Vandient homework. That's good I think. So I'll keep an eye on them, don't worry.'

Alfred came into the house then. He flopped into an armchair, exhausted from a full day on the farm. He looked at his wife and, sensitive to her every mood and emotion — more sensitive than his son — asked, 'What's the matter, woman? You look bloody fretful.'

'Oh, Alfred,' said Ida, suddenly reminded of her worry, tears overflowing her eyes again. She retrieved her handkerchief from her apron pocket to wipe them away. 'Kelpie Turpin's been locked up in prison,' she said.

'What?!'

Both men were shocked. The Turpins were their neighbours on Main Street at the front of the farm. They knew that despite Walter Turpin's well-paid job on the prestigious V-1 Rapid Brynderwyn Tunnel service, the family was always struggling financially. They had eight children, ranging from an infant boy, born about the time Fannie Flitcroft and her baby boy had died, to a twelve-year-old boy called Doral who went to school with Arthur. Kelpie, a gentle and loving mother, who cared for nothing but her children, was helped in their care by her widowed mother who lived with them.

Cyril sat down at the table, which had been set for dinner.

'Tell us about it, Mama,' he said. 'About Kelpie.'

'They told me in the village,' said Ida, somewhat recovered. 'They said the Peacies took her away this morning.'

'But why?' asked Cyril. 'And who's looking after the kids? The baby?'

'Walter's there,' said Ida. 'And, don't forget, her mother lives with them too.'

Cyril nodded, remembering. 'But what happened?'

'Apparently she was on the Point,' said Ida. 'Said she wanted to find a picnic spot to take the kids to on Wednesday after school. For a Christmas day picnic. A treat, you know.'

'What's wrong with that?' asked Alfred from his armchair.

'Yeah, Mama,' said Cyril. 'What did she do wrong?'

'I don't know,' said Ida firmly. 'They said she was trespassing. On the Point. I don't know. That's what everyone's saying. In the shops and that.'

'Trespassing?' Cyril was surprised. 'But Flitcroft Point's public property. A park.' He turned to his father. 'That's right isn't it, Papa?'

'Well, yes and no,' said Alfred from his armchair. He sounded unsure.

'What do you mean, yes and no?' asked a puzzled Cyril. 'It's either yes or no. It is or it isn't. So what is it?'

'It's complicated,' said Alfred. 'I don't know the details.'

'Eh?'

'Ask your grandfather.'

'I will,' said Cyril. 'Where is he anyway?'

'I'll have to wake him up,' said Ida. 'He'll be here in a minute for his dinner. But, son,' she added, 'what about Kelpie?'

'I'll go and sort it out now,' said Cyril. 'Get it out of the way.'

'Your dinner's ready.'

'Keep it warm for me, Mama. I'll have to sort this thing out. Something's not right.'

'Poor Kelpie,' said a worried Ida. 'I've known her all my life. She wouldn't do nothing wrong. And, anyway, she's scared stiff of the Peace.'

'Where is she?' asked Cyril of his mother. 'In the Peace station?'

'I suppose so,' said his mother. 'They said she was in jail so I suppose that's what they meant.'

'Didn't you ask?'

'I didn't think,' said Ida. 'I was so...'

'I'll go up there now,' said Cyril. 'I'll find out what's going on.'

'What about Walter?'

'What about him?'

'Well, he must know what happened.'

'I'll call in and ask him,' said Cyril.

'Don't be too long,' said his mother. 'Your dinner.'

'Hungry,' said Cyril.

'Go get your father,' Ida said to Alfred as Cyril left the room.

5

THE FLITCROFT HOUSE was set against the far western boundary of the farm, facing Main Street and next to the Great Hall which was also on Flitcroft land. Thus it was only a short walk across the street to the Turpins' house and another short walk up to the village centre where the V-Station, the school, and the Peace Station each took up a side of a small square set back from Main Street which served as its fourth boundary.

Cyril was back in just twenty minutes.

'It's nothing,' he said when he returned.

His mother put his dinner on the table. Arthur had been called, and old Enoch had emerged from his bedroom, so the five of them sat down and bowed their heads as Enoch, who sat at the head of the table, said grace, praying to the God of their Christianity.

'Lord our father,' he said, 'we, sitting together, thank you for the gift of nourishment which we share at this table. As you provided for our ancestors in the past may you continue to sustain us throughout our lives. And while we enjoy your gifts may we never forget the many hungry and needy Kiwilanders living in this unhappy land at the mercy of the foreign Vandiers. Amen.'

'Amen,' the others said together.

'Well?' asked Ida of Cyril as she filled three plates and passed them to the men before serving Arthur and then herself.

'It was a misunderstanding,' said Cyril.

'What sort of misunderstanding?'

'They said the young Peacie didn't realize Kelpie was allowed up there. Wasn't doing no harm.'

'Was it Mot-L's father?' asked Arthur, but he wasn't heard.

'Didn't she explain?' asked Ida.

'Her Vandient isn't very good,' said Cyril.

'Yes it is, Grandmama,' insisted Arthur. 'It's good.'

'It *is* good,' said Ida. 'But she's got a Kiwilander accent and some of the Vandiers like to pretend they can't understand her. They do it to me sometimes.'

'Well, that's what they said at the station,' said Cyril. 'The young Peacie thought she was speaking gibberish. That's what they said.'

'Was it Mot-L's father you talked to, Papa?' asked Arthur again.

'No,' said Cyril impatiently. 'Just some Peacie. I don't know who. He had stripes. And, by the way, don't mention that boy.'

'Why would they do that?' asked Alfred, whose own Vandient was good but heavily accented, like many of his generation. 'Pretend to not understand?'

'It seems the arresting young Peacie was new. *Is* new. And he thought she was a mental defective,' said Cyril. 'That's what they said.'

'That's ridiculous!' said Ida. 'Maybe she was speaking English. Trying to explain.'

'Well, if she was, they *definitely* wouldn't understand her,' said Cyril knowing that few Vandiers could understand any English. 'But she told me she tried to explain in Vandient.'

'Anyway, what did he say? The Peacie you spoke to?'

'He said she was being held for questioning,' said Cyril.

'Questioning?' Ida was angry and confused. 'Questioning? Poor innocent Kelpie? Questioning about what?'

Cyril held up his hands defensively. 'Don't take it out on me, Mama,' he said. 'Anyway, he, the senior officer, was patient enough and let her go once she explained it to me and I explained it to him, calmly, in Vandient.'

'So she's not in prison?'

'No. Of course not,' said Cyril. 'I told you. He said it was a misunderstanding. A mistake.'

'It was *no* mistake,' said old Enoch suddenly. He banged his closed fist on the table in anger and stood up. 'No misunderstanding. Not at all.'

The old man's sudden interjection and anger surprised the others.

'I agree, Grandpapa,' said Cyril. 'Sounds fishy. But what can we do?'

'It's all over now, Papa,' said Alfred calmly. 'Kelpie's home with Walter and the children and that's the end of it.'

'It's *not* the end of it,' insisted Enoch, still angry. 'Believe me, it's *not* the end of it. It's just the beginning of it.'

'Beginning of what?' said Cyril to nobody in particular.

'Please, Papa Enoch,' pleaded Ida who was worried about the frail old man's health. 'Don't get upset. It's not worth it.'

'It is *absolutely* worth it,' said Enoch.

The old man was now leaning forward, resting on his knuckles. The others, including Arthur, looked up at him. They had no idea why he should be so angry. What, they wondered, did he know that they didn't?

With nothing but concern for the old man's welfare, knowing that it wasn't good for him to be so stressed, Ida stood up and moved around the table where she gently took his arm and elbow.

'Come along, Papa Enoch,' she said. 'It's nothing really. Nothing to get worked up about.'

'Yes it is, woman,' insisted the old man, although with less passion. 'And the boy,' he said, pointing across the table to Arthur. 'He is consorting with the enemy. Conspiring.'

'What enemy?' asked Ida, shocked at the suggestion of conspiracy by Arthur.

'He's friends with that boy,' said the old man. 'That Vandier boy. He's the son of the Peace Force Superior. How do we know what they talk about in that shed every day?'

'Not *every* day,' protested Arthur.

'Just about every day.'

'Just school days.'

'Just about every day,' repeated the old man.

'But...' Ida was about to defend her grandson when she was interrupted by Cyril.

'I agree with Grandpapa,' he said. 'No more, boy,' he said directly to Arthur. 'You mustn't see that Vandier boy no more.'

'But school's nearly finished now,' said Arthur. 'Till March.'

'School or no school,' said Cyril. 'You'll see no more of that boy.'

'But Papa...' said a shocked Arthur.

But his father held forward and upright the coarse and calloused palm of his right hand. 'I forbid it,' he said. 'No more. Do you understand?'

'Yes, Papa,' said Arthur meekly.

Arthur had no idea why Mot-L was suddenly "the enemy". Nor did he know what he could say to Mot-L.

Or when.

The next day was Tuesday, Christmas Eve. He would *have* to meet him after school, as arranged, and tell him then. Then there was another week of school to go before the summer holidays during which he wouldn't be able to see Mot-L anyway.

Meanwhile, for the diners, the pleasure of the waiting meal was spoiled by the tension at the table which affected them all. Ida, still standing at Enoch's side, holding his elbow, broke the silence and the tension when she gently eased the old man down into his chair saying, 'Just sit down and eat, eh, Papa Enoch. Everything'll be all right.'

The old man complied, albeit reluctantly. 'Cyril's quite right,' he said quietly, looking up at his daughter-in-law. 'About the Vandier boy.'

The family resumed eating in silence.

'Quite right,' he repeated, before himself withdrawing into silence.

But while his voice was silent his remembering mind was busy, racing back to his own boyhood.

6

'WHY DO THEY hate us?' the boy Enoch had once asked his father, the priest.

'What's that, son?' asked a tired and dejected Henri.

'Why do the Vandiers hate us?' the young Enoch asked again.

'They don't hate us,' said Henri.

'Yes they do,' insisted young Enoch. 'They say we are dull and stupid. That we have no culture.'

As a child Enoch was more aware of the Vandiers' attitudes to Kiwilanders than his father who was still — then at least — full of Christian charity and forgiveness.

'They say we are born warriors,' continued Enoch. 'They say that before they came we were just savages engaged in constant wars. They call them "World Wars" because all over the world millions of people were killed.'

'Where did you hear such vulgar things?' asked Henri in disgust. 'You are only, what, eight years old?'

'From the boys who go to school,' said Enoch.

Enoch had refused to go to the new Vandier school — he was taught to read and write English by his clergyman father — and so never learned to speak even a little Vandient. But he did mix and play with children who went to the village school and so learned from them the history they were taught by their Vandier teachers.

'They teach such things at the village school?' asked a shocked Henri. 'To Kiwiland boys and girls?'

'Yes, Papa,' said Enoch. 'And lots more awful things besides. All about us.'

'Oh, dear,' said the worried clergyman.

'So, were we really savages like they say? Were there really those awful wars?'

'Yes, there were wars,' admitted Henri. 'But things were sorted out in our own way. It may not have been always right, my boy, but it was *our* way. We had our language, culture, customs and religion and they were all we needed. They were different from the Vandiers' but that doesn't mean they were inferior or wrong.'

'But they think we *are* inferior and wrong,' said the boy, angry and resentful. 'They really do.'

Now, as old Enoch began eating, silently but resentfully reflecting on the past, he thought again, as he often did, that, since his boyhood, little had changed for his people.

But he wasn't entirely correct. Since his unhappy childhood the Vandiers had softened their opinion; they had come to consider the native Kiwilanders rather kindly, benevolently if rather patronizingly. They now saw them generally as a simple, cheerful, gentle and tolerant people, innocently practising their strange religion — unfortunately riddled with strange but harmless superstitions — and still speaking, between themselves, the old English language despite many Vandier campaigns to render it extinct.

With his vivid memories of the sicknesses, his family's forced flight from their home in Whangārei, the hardships which followed, and the arrival of the Vandiers, old Enoch — now a hundred-and-five years old — had never become reconciled to the new world in which he found himself and in which he had married and raised his only son, Alfred. He suppressed his resentment as best he could, most of the time, but his intolerance of the Vandiers, and what he saw as their domination of the country stolen from its rightful owners, was well known.

His irritability and chauvinism were generally tolerated by his family. They knew he spoke out only on things he considered of utmost importance to the welfare of his people. And so, with this rare outburst of anger from his now-quiet grandfather, Cyril Flitcroft guessed — correctly as it turned out — that there was more to Kelpie Turpin's arrest than a mere "misunderstanding". More, perhaps, than the Peace Force was letting on.

More trouble was to come. Of that he was certain.

*

As with Easter and always, Christmas came and went quietly; the villagers had no desire to draw the Vandiers' attention to their Christian traditions and rituals.

There *were* family celebrations: the traditional exchange of gifts in the early morning and a special roast turkey or goose dinner in the evening. The only public observance came late on Christmas night when some of the more devout villagers gathered in the churchyard, in front of the church, on the Flitcroft Beach side; the church itself was too small to accommodate a large congregation. Holding lighted candles, they listened as old Enoch, standing in the church porch, read the Christmas story from the holy book he had inherited from his father. They sang hymns and carols too; ancient songs which had been passed down to them through the generations.

Enoch managed to stand unaided during the Christmas night service, and his voice was still steady and strong, but his daughter-in-law, Ida, wasn't alone in thinking that the old man looked frailer, less steady on his feet, than he had at Fannie's funeral in May.

In the week following Christmas outside observers might have thought life in Flitcroft village was no different from any other week, but they would have been mistaken. Apart from the obvious fact that summer had arrived — which meant more hours on the land complemented, at least and fortunately, by pleasant leisure hours in the extended evenings — the villagers, young and old, while evidently going about their daily routines, were quietly and secretly excited in anticipation of the New Year's Eve celebration.

Meanwhile, Arthur didn't see Mot-L again. His friend simply stopped coming. Arthur didn't know why but was somewhat relieved that he wouldn't have to confess that his father had banned their meetings.

7

THE NEW YEAR'S Eve party on Flitcroft Point was a tradition as old as the village.

Preparations began when the current chairman of the village council — in this case, Hugh Wombourne, the village barber — was despatched to Whangārei during the week to perform his last official duty: to buy a selection of the best and most spectacular Vandier pyrotechnics which would be set off on the stroke of midnight, on the year's last day, at which moment he would be replaced by the chairman-elect for the new year.

Meanwhile, youths who could be spared from their work on the land were detailed to collect dry wood from Flitcroft Beach and from the bush high at the back of the Point with which to build a bonfire on the Flitcroft Point plateau. Women at home prepared food for the night while those men skilled at brewing the village's strong ale took up barrels of the stuff which they set up in a special marquee from which the women and children were excluded.

It was because children were not allowed into the men's beer marquee that Arthur wasn't able to immediately tell his father what he and Doral Turpin had seen in the dark, high at the bushline, beyond the edge of the party.

*

The next morning, the first day of that fateful year, 2177, Arthur was forbidden by his grandmother to disturb the men.

'They're sleeping,' she said at breakfast. 'They had a big night last night.'

'I know, Grandmama,' said Arthur. 'But...'

'They work hard all year, boy,' said Ida sharply. 'They're entitled.'

'I know,' said Arthur, resigned.

They were joined then by old Enoch who had spent the night in the beer marquee with the other men, but for the company rather than the drink.

He sat down.

'You all right, Papa Enoch?' Ida asked the old man as she served him his breakfast.

'I'm fine, lass,' he replied. 'Better than those other two,' he added with a chuckle.

Ida raised her eyebrows with a smile.

'Great-Grandpapa?' asked Arthur suddenly.

'What is it, lad?'

'Last night, at the Point, I saw something. Something strange.'

'Don't bother your Great-Grandpapa, boy,' said Ida.

'But I must tell someone,' said Arthur. 'And Papa and Grandpapa are both asleep.'

'Let him talk, lass,' said Enoch. 'What is it, lad? What did you see?'

'Last night, with Doral...'

Enoch looked questioningly at Ida.

'Doral Turpin,' explained Ida. 'His mother Kelpie's the one got arrested by the Peacies.'

'Oh, yes,' said Enoch with a frown. 'So, lad, what did you see?'

'Lines, Great-Grandpapa,' said Arthur. 'Lines. Lots of them.'

Old Enoch leaned back and turned his head to better catch what Arthur was saying. 'What do you mean, lad?' he asked. 'Lines? What sort of lines?'

'Lines. Painted on the grass. With white paint.'

The old man looked somewhat alarmed. He looked up at Ida, who wasn't really listening, and then back to Arthur. 'Where was this?' he asked.

'Up at the very top of Flitcroft Point where it slopes up. Where the grass stops and the bush starts,' said Arthur. 'You know where I mean, Great-Grandpapa?'

'I know exactly where you mean,' said Enoch who had known Flitcroft Point when it was still part of the Flitcroft farm when he was a boy.

Suddenly Ida paid attention. 'That's where the old houses used to be, isn't it Papa Enoch?' she asked. 'Up there? The ones that got burned down?'

'That's exactly it, lass,' said Enoch. 'Exactly.' And then, turning to Arthur, he asked: 'And when was this again, lad?'

'I told you, Great-Grandpapa,' insisted Arthur. 'Last night. At the big bonfire. Doral took me there and showed me.'

'Why did he take you way up there, so far from the party?'

'He said his mother told him about the lines,' said Arthur. 'His mother thinks they've got something to do with her being arrested and that. So Doral wanted to see them for himself.'

'She didn't tell Cyril about no lines,' said Enoch to Ida. 'Did she?'

Ida shook her head slowly and said, 'He never said nothing about no lines.'

Enoch turned back to Arthur. 'And that's where you saw these white lines?' he asked.

'Yes.'

'Last night? How could you see up there? In the dark?'

'We could see,' said Arthur. 'There was the moon, and the light from the bonfire.'

Enoch leaned forward, resting one elbow on the table. He stared hard at his great-grandson and asked, slowly and carefully, 'So, lad, think carefully and tell me more about these lines. Exactly what did they look like?'

'They were just lines, Great-Grandpapa. Long white lines painted on the grass.'

'Just straight lines?' probed Enoch.

'They made squares and rectangles too.'

'I see,' said Enoch as though that confirmed something. 'How big were these squares and rectangles? Could you tell?'

'I don't know,' said Arthur. 'They were pretty big.'

'As big as all this house?'

'Bigger,' said Arthur without hesitation. 'Much bigger.'

'I see,' said Enoch.

'What is it, Papa Enoch?' asked Ida who could tell that the old man was worried about something. 'Do you know what it's all about?'

'I do, lass,' said the old man who had seen such lines before. He was shaking his head slowly and — thought Ida — ominously.

'And?'

Arthur was as attentive as his grandmother, waiting anxiously for the old man's response. But they were not to be satisfied. All Enoch said, and quietly, was, 'We need to talk to Alfred and Cyril.'

January the first became January the second before Alfred and Cyril returned from their night-time investigation of the lines high on Flitcroft Point. Despite the hour, old Enoch was still awake — albeit dozing in his armchair — when they returned.

The night was warm and fine, and the moon was still bright, so the investigators didn't need the torches they had taken to discover in detail what Arthur had described only broadly. For the sake of accuracy they had taken one of the farm's fencing tape measures to determine the dimensions of a few of the squares and rectangles which they recorded in a notebook, together with a rough plan of the whole site of which their sampling measurements were typical.

Once back at the house, in the still-dark hours of early morning, they cut a big sheet of paper from Ida's butcher's roll which they spread out on the kitchen table. Enoch then watched and waited as Alfred and Cyril worked together, referring to their measurement notes, and the small plan they had roughly sketched by moonlight, to draw out an accurate plan of the entire site showing all the white lines and rectangles to scale.

'That's it, Grandpapa,' said Cyril standing back from the table, satisfied with the night's work. 'Just like you wanted.'

'Not what I *wanted*, lad,' said the old man.

'But Papa,' protested Alfred, 'you said...'

'I said I *needed* to see something better than the boy described,' said Enoch. 'But it is, as I feared, something I never *wanted* to see.'

The three men went to bed that morning truly shocked by what Alfred and Cyril's plan had revealed. But more — and worse — was to come when they woke, tired and late, the next morning.

THE FLITCROFT VILLAGE council was moribund; it served little purpose. Its chairmanship was therefore largely ceremonial, a role awarded to each councillor in turn for the term of one year.

The chairman for the new year was Oscar Bladen, the village undertaker, who lived above his business on Main Street with his wife and two children. He was a jolly fellow in his forties who was universally liked, despite his profession, and who, as the new year began, was looking forward to the fun and fellowship associated with his few non-onerous chairmanship duties.

He was shocked, therefore, when, early on the Thursday morning following the first day of his chairmanship, he was visited by the Superior of the Peace Force accompanied by two of his officers and a young woman who identified herself as a senior magistrate.

They were there — so the frightened and perplexed Oscar Bladen was informed — to serve him, as the current chairman of the Flitcroft village council, with notice that, the magistrate read from the official document, '... the government requires and is hereby taking as of this day dated part of that strip of land between the east boundary of the Flitcroft farm and the beach, known locally as Flitcroft Beach, at low tide from its northern limit where it meets Beach Street and joins the government land, known locally as Flitcroft Point, south to the boundary of the village cemetery and church.'

The whole conversation was, of course, in Vandient, as was the official printed notice which, having been read aloud by the magistrate, was re-rolled and duly handed to the bewildered chairman.

'I don't understand,' said Oscar Bladen as he received it. 'Can you take it just like that? Our land?'

'*I* can't,' said the young woman magistrate pedantically, 'but the government can. For legitimate government purposes, of course.'

Oscar looked and was speechless.

'The village council will be notified about financial compensation in due course,' the magistrate added.

Deep in the backlands, an old poultry farmer had died suddenly while chasing and strangling geese for the Whangārei market. It took Oscar Bladen a full day to go so far inland to recover the body and bring it back to prepare it for burial. It was, therefore, early evening before he was able to call to the Flitcroft farm to inform Cyril — his friend, confidant and fellow village councillor — of his visit from the young lady magistrate.

The Flitcrofts were sitting down to dinner when Oscar called, but despite their hunger, after a full day's work under the hot summer sun, Cyril and Alfred agreed to set aside their eating to hear what an obviously anxious Oscar needed to say.

And so, standing while the family remained sitting, Oscar told his story.

'And then what?' asked Cyril when Oscar had finished.

'They just left,' said Oscar. 'Left me to it. Standing there like a dummy.' He shrugged. 'I didn't know what to say or do.'

'There must be more to it than that,' said Alfred.

'Oh, yes,' said Oscar suddenly remembering. He reached into his trouser pocket and withdrew a rolled piece of coarse parchment-like paper. 'They gave me this.'

'Show me,' said Cyril.

He took it, looked at it, and tossed it on the table with disgust. 'Official Vandient,' he said.

'Papa,' said Arthur suddenly. 'Let me see.'

'You can *read* this sort of Vandient? Officialese?'

'I've been meaning to tell you...' said Ida.

Cyril raised his eyebrows, surprised not only at his son's ability but also that he wasn't aware of it.

'A bit,' said Arthur modestly, as his grandmother took the document from the table and handed it to him.

Arthur took it, unrolled it, scanned it quickly, looked up at the five adults whose eyes were fixed on him in wonder, and said, 'It's not much, pretty short, and I don't understand all the words exactly, but...'

'Just tell us, boy,' said Cyril impatiently.

'Well, it pretty well says, in government-style language, what Mr Bladen just said. What they said to him.'

'What's that, boy? *You* say it. From the paper. In English.'

'It says,' said Arthur, translating to English slowly from the official document, 'that the government requires and is hereby taking — as of this day dated, it says — I suppose that's today,' Arthur looked up to his father for guidance.

'That's today all right,' interrupted Alfred.

'Go on, boy,' Cyril said.

'Where was I?' said Arthur returning his attention to the document. 'Ah, here. It says, all that strip of land between the east boundary of the Flitcroft farm — that's *our* farm, Papa — and the beach, known locally as Flitcroft Beach, that bit's in brackets,' he added, 'at low tide from its northern limit where it meets Beach Street and joins the government land, known locally as Flitcroft Point, that bit's also in brackets,' he said again, 'south to the boundary of the village cemetery and church.'

'What's all that mean?' asked Enoch

'It means they're taking all the beach land except the church land and the cemetery,' said Arthur mechanically. At that moment he could think only of his dead mother and baby brother lying together in said cemetery.

'Bloody generous of them,' said Alfred. 'But I can't believe it. The beach land.'

'Except the church land and cemetery,' said Arthur again.

Ida and Cyril simply shook their heads in wonder and puzzlement. Oscar, standing alone at the end of the room, merely looked on dumbly. Arthur didn't know what to say or think and so he simply leaned forward and laid the official government document on the table.

Enoch, though, was not speechless. Rather, he pushed back his chair, stood up and said, 'I've seen this coming for years.'

'Sit down, *please,* Papa Enoch,' said Ida firmly. 'Sit down before you fall down.'

'No, lass,' said the old man loudly. 'I *must* talk.'

His sudden interruption was so uncharacteristically insistent that the meeting went silent as all those present turned to look at the old man.

'I must tell you,' said Enoch. 'That Kelpie Turpin business, getting arrested on Flitcroft Point, that was just the beginning.'

'Beginning of what?' asked Ida.

'Believe me,' said the old man. 'I told Cyril and Alfred last night.'

He retrieved Cyril and Alfred's map of white lines from the dresser, where they had stored it, and spread it out on the table.

'There,' he said. 'The lines. Now, do you know what they are?'

Oscar Bladen, Ida and Arthur shook their heads as Cyril and Alfred looked on.

'Well *we* do,' said the old man, waving a finger between Alfred and Cyril. 'And now this.' He pointed to the official Vandier document still lying on the table. 'More of the same.'

The others really *were* listening now.

'I'll tell you, lad,' said Enoch directly to Oscar Bladen. 'I think you should call an urgent village meeting.'

'A council meeting?' asked Oscar. 'But Mr Flitcroft, I've never done that before. I mean, I'm new to this. My second day.'

'No, lad,' said Enoch emphatically. 'The whole village needs to hear about this. *And* about what I have to say. *Must* say. The whole village, do you understand?'

'The Great Hall?' asked Oscar.

'The Great Hall,' said Enoch. 'And the sooner the better.'

9

'YES, OF COURSE you can come,' said Cyril. 'You *should* come. But you better sit at the back.'

'I'll sit with Doral,' said Arthur.

The Great Hall was not great enough to accommodate the whole attending crowd but it was a warm evening so people were happy to stand outside listening through the wide-open windows. None knew why the meeting had been called, nor what it was about, but they all were sufficiently respectful of the Flitcroft family, and of old Enoch in particular, to assume that, whatever the matter to be discussed, it would be important.

The members of the village council sat together in a row to one side of the stage. As they arrived and took their places they projected an air of knowing self-importance. There were seven of them, including the chairman, Oscar Bladen, although of all of them only Oscar and Cyril Flitcroft knew the purpose of the meeting. And none but Alfred Flitcroft, who sat below the stage in the front row, and old Enoch, who sat on his own at the front and centre of the stage, knew what Cyril intended to propose at the end of the meeting.

The introduction by Oscar Bladen was brief. He stood up to make it, moving forward to stand on

Enoch's left, his right hand resting on the back of the old man's chair.

'Ladies and gentlemen,' he said. 'Thank you for your attendance tonight. We've called this urgent meeting because your council here...' he had a couple of pieces of paper in his left hand which he waved to indicate the councillors sitting behind him to his left '... has grave concerns about the integrity of the village's lands.'

'What does that mean?' came a shout from the floor of the hall. 'Integrity of our lands? Speak English, Oscar. Plain English.'

'Thank you, Nigel,' said Oscar, acknowledging the questioner. 'It means we're afraid the government is taking more and more of the village's traditional land.'

'What do you mean, afraid?' came another question from the floor.

A murmur of general agreement immediately filled the Great Hall.

Oscar held up his left hand, in which he was holding the papers, for quiet. 'Please!' he insisted. 'Hear us out. One step at a time, eh, and you'll see what we mean.'

The meeting went quiet with expectation.

Oscar continued: 'All right,' he said. 'To put it plainly, the government *is* taking — I mean actually *has* taken — the village's beachfront land from...'

At this point the shouts of anger and protest were so loud that Oscar was unable to continue.

'Please! Please!' he shouted, waving his outstretched arms, palms down, in an attempt to promote calm.

A reluctant quiet settled on the meeting eventually until someone shouted, loudly and angrily, 'What the hell's going on, Oscar? Tell us what's going on.'

The audience again erupted in noisy protest.

'That's exactly what I'm trying to do,' said Oscar to a now restless audience. 'If only...'

'Go on then!' called a woman from the back of the hall.

So Oscar Bladen told them all, as plainly and briefly as he could, of the visit he had received from the important lady magistrate, supported by the Superior of the Peace Force and a couple of his staff.

He then held up the official document in one hand.

'Let me read from the official notice they gave me. So you can hear it for yourselves.'

He read from the English translation which Arthur had written out for him.

'This is to inform you,' he read, 'that the government requires and is hereby taking as of this day dated — that's as of yesterday —' he inserted, 'part of that strip of land between the east boundary of the Flitcroft farm and the beach — known locally as Flitcroft Beach it says — at low tide from its northern limit where it meets Beach Street and joins the government land — and here it says known locally as Flitcroft Point — south to the boundary of the village cemetery and church.'

He stopped there, dropped his paper-holding hand to his side, and looked blankly out at the outraged audience.

Most people immediately understood the implications of the notice; those who didn't were soon made to understand by their neighbours.

Many questions were then fired at Oscar from the floor. Indeed, the meeting became loud and utterly disorderly. Oscar and Cyril had not only expected the villagers' angry reaction but were together astute enough to distil the general anger and shouting to two essential questions which Oscar set about answering at once.

The first concerned the church and cemetery.

'You heard clearly enough what was plainly written,' said Oscar holding up the official document again. 'The village keeps total ownership of the church land and cemetery right up to the cemetery boundary fence.'

The second concerned financial compensation.

'She said the government will notify the council about payment in due course.'

'It's not in the official bit of paper, though, is it,' shouted a male voice.

'No, it's not, I must admit,' said Oscar. 'But I'm sure they'll pay, in due course, as the magistrate lady said.'

The crowd booed quietly then.

'And when we know what it's all about we — the council I mean — we'll let everyone know.'

At which the other seated councillors all nodded sagely although none but Cyril knew that when the government last took village land — when it appropriated the whole of Flitcroft Point from the village in 2089 — the compensation was what Enoch had insisted was "derisory". Enoch had told him that many times, a fact that Cyril had found recorded in the village council minutes stored in the church.

He also knew — and he thought others of his age and older would remember — how the government reneged on its promise of more village housing when it evicted those few village residents remaining on Flitcroft Point and demolished and burned down their houses; that was only twenty-five years ago, in 2151. And so he sympathized with the mood of the meeting, as did Oscar. But there was more to come and Cyril wanted to wait until his grandfather, Enoch, had spoken before he revealed either his total scepticism about the government's promises or his plan.

'Now, we're not finished yet,' said Oscar.

The men on the stage — including Enoch, who was waiting his turn to speak — all sensed that the mood of the meeting had turned sour and decidedly unpleasant. The audience was seething with anger and impatience, that much was clear, but there was also an over-riding feeling of frustration and impotence; of having no idea what they could do against the power of central government.

They were, in fact, silently begging for guidance and leadership.

'I know how angry you are,' continued the chairman. 'How frustrating all this is. What are we going to do? you ask. But, as I say, we're not finished yet. There are other matters related to this whole affair which we have to consider. So, first, we need to hear from Walter Turpin.'

Walter stood up hesitantly, nervously.

'You all know Walter,' said Oscar. He turned to the seated councillors. 'So, Walter, over to you.'

The meeting politely applauded Walter Turpin as he stepped forward and Oscar returned to his seat.

10

WALTER TURPIN WAS liked and respected in the village, but he was not a good speaker. He was nervous, spoke too quietly, often had to repeat himself with more volume, and was not truly convincing in describing the circumstances of his wife's arrest for simply exploring the upper reaches of Flitcroft Point in search of a picnic spot. His son, Doral, sitting with Arthur at the back of the room, cringed with embarrassment for his hapless father.

Seeing Walter losing the attention of the meeting forced Cyril to join his friend at the front of the stage. Walter looked hugely relieved that his speaking duties were over; he returned meekly to his seated place with the other councillors leaving Cyril to continue.

'The thing is,' said Cyril loudly, commandingly, 'when I went to the Peace Station to find out why Walter's wife was arrested, about what was going on, they said that the young Peacie had made a mistake. And so they apologized and let Kelpie go as soon as I explained what she was so innocently doing up there. But, as you'll see, as you'll hear...' and here Cyril paused for emphasis '... we think the only mistake the Peacie made was actually doing his duty.

'He actually did what he was supposed to do: keep villagers away from the area. But if he'd known better he'd have used his discretion, his initiative, and let Kelpie go about what she was doing, harmlessly looking for a picnic spot. Instead he mindlessly followed orders and so drew attention, *our* attention, to what's *really* going on up there. What the government's trying to hide.'

It was a long speech but it didn't satisfy the listeners. Rather, it merely aroused their curiosity.

'So what *is* going up there, then?' came a shout from the floor.

'Yeah, Cyril. What are they trying to hide?' came another.

Cyril held forward the palm of his hand, asking for patience.

'We *do* know what they're trying to hide,' he said, 'and we'll come back to that. But first I want you to hear some important background from my grandfather here.'

The meeting applauded as Cyril introduced old Enoch. But it was merely a courtesy. While the people undoubtedly respected Enoch Flitcroft they were, on this occasion, less concerned with his status in the village and more concerned — anxious — to hear what he had to say and how it was related to the problem at hand. After the brief polite applause the audience immediately went quiet knowing that the old man would, out of necessity, speak softly.

Cyril stepped back only a pace.

Enoch stood up to speak but immediately changed his mind and sat down.

He spoke quietly, as expected, and the audience strained to hear him. But they listened carefully because they knew that no one knew more of the village's history than old man Flitcroft.

'Remember,' said Enoch, 'that in 2080 — nearly a hundred years ago — my uncle and my father granted that whole strip of their Flitcroft farmland along the beach to the village for common use. It's on that land where the church still stands — my father's church which he and the villagers built — and the cemetery where he, my father Henri, lies, as well as his father and mother, his wife and my mother Catherine, my two sisters and their menfolk and children, my uncle and his wife who welcomed us into their home after the sicknesses, my own wife, Violet, and, lately, my great-grandson's poor dear mother who was only young and who herself, as a child, had been sadly orphaned.'

Mention of his mother caught Arthur's attention and so he listened even more carefully as the old man talked on in his somewhat monotonous fashion.

'Remember, too,' continued the old man, 'as well as the beach land now being taken by order of that hateful document...' he indicated to the councillors sitting behind him to his left, at which Oscar Bladen held up and waved the document in question '...my uncle, supported by my father, also granted the whole of Flitcroft Point, such valuable pasture back then, to the village. As I said, that was way back in 2080. I was just nine years old but I remember it well. There are big views of the ocean up there. Up where Kelpie Turpin was arrested the day before Christmas. So the villagers built new houses there, at the back, in front of the bush, for the people. And the rest was meant as a park for the village.'

'So, what's this all about, Mr Flitcroft?' came a question from the floor.

'I'll tell you what it's about, lad,' said the old man. 'Just nine years later, in 2089, the government said they needed it all, the whole of Flitcroft Point. They needed it. And so they took it. All of it. Just like...' he made a snap in the air with his thumb and big finger '... that!

'Just like they're taking our beach land now,' he added.

Cyril, who was still standing a pace or so behind and beside his grandfather, said to the audience: 'Remember, they paid the village council, but...'

'That's right,' interrupted Enoch. 'Just like they say they'll pay for the beach land. But it took ages to get the money and then, when they finally paid, it was such a derisory amount. A pittance. An insult.'

Cyril, looking down into the hall, realized, from the general reaction of the audience, the murmuring, the number of heads shaking in disbelief, that the villagers hadn't heard this story before.

'They cheated us,' he said loudly. He was interrupting his grandfather but he couldn't help it. 'They took *our* land. They kept it. Paid a pittance. And now they're doing it again.'

'Why did they take it?' came a question from the floor.

'Because of the Americans,' said Enoch.

Arthur, at the back of the hall, was puzzled; this was another story he'd never heard before.

'Back then, you see,' continued the old man, 'America was a great and powerful country and the government thought they, the Americans, were going to invade Kiwiland. So they wanted Flitcroft Point, and lots of other places, too, to build forts. Something like that. Big weapons of defence, maybe. I don't know exactly.'

'But there's no fort or weapons or nothing at the Point,' shouted someone from the floor.

'Exactly!' said Enoch sounding contemptuous. 'It was a complete ruse by the government to take Flitcroft Point.'

11

THE OLD MAN wasn't entirely correct; it wasn't altogether a ruse.

At that time the government felt justified in fearing an American invasion. They thought the once-all-powerful Americans, still recovering from the sicknesses, would seek to conquer lands considered empty, including Kiwiland, and so wanted to establish defensive positions up and down the east coast.

What the government didn't know was that America was powerless.

When the sicknesses came the American people suffered more than most. Their nation was both fanatically religious and morally corrupt, riven with racial hatred, and with many more lethal weapons than people. And so, over the course of those long-ago years, the fifty-three states, unable to agree on almost anything, fractured into five factions, each with its own interests. The civil wars which followed caused the deaths of many more millions of people above the many millions who had already died from the returning viruses and famines which were then followed by a series of catastrophic earthquakes.

The once-powerful United States of America was no longer powerful or united.

A shouted question: 'So when was that, Mr Flitcroft?'

Enoch, somewhat exhausted from his speech, and disappointed about how little his audience knew, surveyed the mass of anxious faces looking up at him with a resigned sigh of sadness.

'I remember it well,' he said. 'Twenty eighty-nine it was. I was eighteen. The year the government took Flitcroft Point from the people.'

'The thing is,' interrupted Cyril, stepping forward, 'we're foolish enough to think it's still a park. *Our* park. But it's not.'

'Who remembers the houses that were there?' asked Enoch rhetorically. 'They've all gone haven't they. That was just a few years ago. The people were evicted by the government and their houses were all burned down.'

'But they built us new houses,' called out a woman. 'In the village. We live in one. It's good.'

'But we were promised more, weren't we,' said Enoch. 'But what happened? Absolutely nothing.'

'That's right,' called out an old lady who was standing at the back. 'Me and Charlie got chucked out then. Left homeless.'

'So what did you do, Maud?' asked Cyril who recognized the speaker.

'Moved in with Charlie's brother,' was the reply. 'And we're still there.'

'We can still *use* the park, though,' came another shout, a man's voice this time.

'Oh, yes, Humphrey,' said Enoch who recognized the voice of Humphrey Kent, the manager of the village slaughterhouse. 'They let us think that. But what happened to Kelpie Turpin? What's that about? It's *their* land, remember. Their land by *their* laws. They took it and they can do whatever they like, including arresting an innocent lady looking for a picnic place. And now, believe me...' the old man paused ominously and held up one crooked forefinger by way of an imminent warning '...there's more to come.'

Cyril stepped forward.

'We now come to the point of this meeting,' he said. 'You see, the thing is, during the night of the New Year's Eve party on Flitcroft Point a couple of village boys wandered up to the bushline — up where Kelpie Turpin was arrested — and found some strange white lines that were painted there on the grass.'

Cyril now had the audience's full attention.

'They could see them clearly in the moonlight,' he continued. 'So, at the urging of my grandfather, who thought he knew what the lines were all about, we — that is my father and me — we went up there late on Wednesday night. Early Thursday morning, really. We figured out that there must be Peacies hiding in the bush up there during the day. But not at night. The moon was still bright enough that we could see the lines for ourselves. We came back, told my grandfather what we had seen, described them, and he told us then, for sure, what they were. What they meant.'

'Come on, Cyril,' came a shout from the floor; it was Humphrey Kent again. 'What's it all about?'

'My grandfather said he's seen those sorts of lines before,' said Cyril. 'Believe it or not, those lines are marking out sections for houses. And, going by the size of the sections, they're going to be big, expensive, luxurious houses with big views down Flitcroft Point and out to sea.'

The meeting was shocked into silence.

Even Oscar Bladen and most of the other councillors were taken by surprise by this information which Cyril had kept between himself, his father and grandfather. But one, Primus Townend, who was a leading hand at a sawmill in Whangārei, stood up then and came forward to join Cyril.

'There's a lot of timber coming in from up north,' he said to Cyril and the meeting. 'We were told by the high-ups that there's a big housing project coming up. I never guessed...'

'See,' said Cyril to the silent hall. 'That'll be it all right.'

Primus was shaking his head in disbelief. 'I never thought...' he turned to Cyril, clearly upset, and said, 'I'm so sorry, Cyril...' and then, turning to the audience '... everyone. I just thought, well,

I don't know what I thought but I never thought of this happening.'

The chairman stood up and came forward then to stand beside the two other men and the seated Enoch.

'What else might you know, Primus?' asked Oscar seriously.

'When we asked — and there are others here who can back me up about this, right, boys? — when we asked they said there'd be a lot of big houses for rich people which meant not only lots of building and construction and labouring work but then lots of jobs for servants and cooks and maids and gardeners and things like that. They made it sound really good for us. For employment. But I thought — we all thought — it was planned for Dargaville. So much good land over there.'

'It's true,' shouted a man from the floor. 'I work at the mill too. With Primus. I heard the same thing.'

'So you see,' said Cyril to the meeting, 'that's why they've taken the beach land. So the owners of all those big luxury houses on the Point will have access to the beach. So, believe you me, by the time this is over we won't have access to Flitcroft Point at all.'

'What the hell are we going to do?' asked a still shocked and upset Primus Townend of nobody in particular.

'Well, this is what *I* think we should do,' said Cyril.

12

THE MEETING WAS unanimous in adopting Cyril Flitcroft's plan.

However, by eight o'clock the next morning only about thirty villagers had turned up on the plateau, the large flat area high in the middle of Flitcroft Point. But those there, a mix of men and women, a few married couples and some children, were not only keen to get started but were quick to allay Cyril's disappointment.

'It'll grow, Cyril,' they said. 'People have jobs in Whangārei, and the backlanders have to make arrangements for their animals and gardens. Not everyone can be here at the drop of a hat. And not all the time. But they will come. They really will.'

And so they did.

It was to be what old Enoch recalled from history and referred to variously as non-violent protest, peaceful protest, civil disobedience. The idea, sown by the old man but acted upon and led by his grandson, Cyril, was to occupy Flitcroft Point with so many people that prospective purchasers would be discouraged from buying land and building there. Cyril knew that contractors and prospective residents wouldn't want to engage in unpleasantness with the local people; indeed, he guessed that most Vandiers knew or suspected that the Kiwilanders had a moral right to the land's ownership.

He also knew that even if the Flitcroft Point sections *were* sold as planned the occupation would make it hard if not impossible for contractors to bring in the machinery, equipment and materials required to build houses there. And, anyway, he had been assured by his fellow councillor, Hugh Wombourne, who owned the village barbershop and was therefore familiar with the moods and attitudes of the village's labouring men, that the workers and tradesmen upon whom the builders and contractors relied would risk unemployment rather than contribute their labour to the housing projects planned for Flitcroft Point.

'Me and my staff will spread the word,' he said to Cyril.

The powerful Kiwiland Labour Council also promised support.

'Don't worry,' said the council's president. 'They won't be able to do nothing without our members. They'll be absolutely stuffed.'

Nevertheless, on that first day of protest Cyril was disappointed with the turnout. Nothing was achieved and the daylight hours were spent merely sitting in the sun discussing what *might* happen; what *might* be achieved. By the end of the day Cyril was depressed and despondent.

He was there with his father while Arthur played with the few other children including Doral Turpin whose father spent as much time there as he could. Kelpie Turpin arrived at the site at noontime, with Ida Flitcroft, with enough sandwiches and drinks to satisfy the hunger and thirst of the pioneering protesters. They returned just before sunset with tureens of hot stew and buttered bread.

It was then, as they sat around a fire enjoying their hot meal, that Arthur, who was sitting cross-legged looking up to the distant bush behind which the sun was setting, saw three uniformed Peace Officers emerge from the bush and make their way along the edge of the bushline obviously on their way back to the village Peace Station.

'They must have been there all day,' said Cyril.

'*Every* bloody day, I bet,' said Alfred.

'We're not doing nothing wrong,' said Ida. 'They can't do nothing to us.'

'They wouldn't bloody dare,' said Alfred cockily.

Cyril, Alfred and Arthur spent that first night in the tent they had brought. A few others had also brought tents and that first day of occupation on Flitcroft Point ended with a small cluster of tents of various sizes, shapes and quality, glowing for a while from the lamps which burned inside them, offering comfort to the nervous protesters who eventually fell asleep from exhaustion.

*

Early next morning the campers on Flitcroft Point — tired from lack of sleep and anxiety — were awakened early, very early, by many excited voices.

As Cyril emerged from his tent, shading his eyes from the brightness of the sun rising in a pale blue sky over the vast Pacific Ocean, the doubt, disappointment and despondency of the previous day gave way first to relief and then elation. The excited voices which had woken him and the other campers were those of a procession of villagers — dozens of them — traipsing up the slope from Beach Street bearing tents and sleeping bags and food and he didn't know what else.

'Will you look at that, Papa,' he said to Alfred, standing at his side.

'I told you, son,' replied his father. 'People needed time to get organized, that's all.'

'It's going to work, isn't it.'

'Bloody oath,' said Alfred. 'But, also, look at that,' he added.

Alfred pointed out what Cyril had just seen for himself: three uniformed Peace Officers walking along the distant bushline, in plain sight, to take up their positions observing the planned building sites and now, incidentally, watching the camp materialising on the plateau below.

'They're not worried about hiding no more,' said Cyril.

'But they're not doing nothing neither,' said Alfred.

'They're being patient,' said Cyril. 'They don't think we'll be here for long.'

'They've got another bloody think coming then, haven't they,' said Alfred.

Cyril merely smiled and moved forward to welcome the new arrivals.

Cyril was right of course. The Peace Force was merely acting on instructions from the government which believed that the protest by occupation, while understandable, would not last long. It knew that the Flitcroft villagers depended on their businesses in the village, or their jobs there and in Whangārei, and that the backlanders had inescapable commitments to their farms, gardens and orchards. It knew that, with limited cash reserves and few other resources, the protesters would have little alternative but to attend first and mostly to those activities which brought the money they needed to support themselves and their families.

It was obvious, therefore, that official government policy was to be patient; to simply watch and wait, certain that the Kiwilanders would sooner or later — probably sooner and certainly with the arrival of winter — tire of their protest and meekly return to the security of routine farm and village life.

While the government was right in believing that the protesters' businesses, farms, animals, poultry, gardens and orchards couldn't be left unattended for long, it was wrong in its estimation of the Kiwilanders' determination to never again surrender to the government's wealth and power.

Over the days and weeks which followed, the growing number of protesters not only organized their camping arrangements but also worked together to protect their income and the welfare of their families. Work-sharing rosters were drawn up to ensure that no farm or business was neglected, that livelihoods and incomes were protected, while the occupation camp was never empty.

At first, when the campers were few, and before the kitchens were organized, the women of the village combined to prepare and deliver food, hot and cold, to be shared amongst the busy workers.

The large marquee which was always erected on the same site for the New Year's Eve party, and had only just been taken down, was set up again as a communal hall for dining and camp meetings. However, as it was decided from the beginning that no alcohol or drugs would be permitted anywhere in the camp, the marquee's traditional role as a *de facto* tavern was renounced and forgotten.

13

AT FIRST, MOST of the village children played around the camp during the long summer days, whether or not their parents were part of the protest. A few, including Arthur, stayed overnight, although most went home at the end of the day, being cared for there by a parent or grandparent, or taken into a crèche supervised by a willing volunteer.

When March arrived the children returned to school. Cyril was adamant that they should and, in this, he was supported by the parents if not by the children themselves. However, the members of the village council were somewhat apprehensive about the children returning to school. They thought it possible — even probable — that the innocent and unknowing children would be quizzed by the teachers about the occupation, its leaders, objectives, and plans, or be otherwise pressured or embarrassed. That one of the teachers was the wife of the Superior of the Peace Force gave them special cause to worry.

However, after the first day of school, and for weeks thereafter, Arthur was able to reassure his father that the subject of the occupation was never mentioned at school, not even obliquely.

'It's completely normal at school,' he told his father. 'It's like all this here doesn't even exist.'

Cyril was relieved, especially when he heard that other parents had received the same assurances from their children.

'And you're not seeing that Vandier boy no more?' asked Cyril.

'I told you, Papa,' said Arthur. 'I didn't see him all summer. He goes to a special posh Vandier school in Whangārei so I *never* see him.'

It was true that Arthur hadn't seen Mot-L during the holidays. But early in the school year there was some indirect contact to which he didn't confess.

'I was home doing the washing yesterday afternoon,' said his grandmother one Saturday when Arthur was home for a bath, 'and your friend Mot-L came to see you.'

'When?'

'After school it was,' said Ida. 'I told him you weren't here.'

'I was up at the Point with Papa.'

'I know. Just as well, too,' said Ida. 'If your father...'

'What did he say?' interrupted Arthur. 'What did he want?'

'I tell you what, boy,' said Ida, 'he speaks pretty good English.'

'I told you, Grandmama. He always wanted to learn English. Now he's good.'

'I've never heard no Vandier ever speak English that good,' said Ida. 'Let alone a child.' She was genuinely surprised and impressed.

'I told you,' said Arthur again. 'He's really clever.'

'I can see that.'

'And nice.'

'I can see that too, boy,' said Ida kindly.

'But what did he want, Grandmama?'

'He asked me to tell you that he's not allowed to see you no more,' said Ida. 'After school or any time.'

'I guessed that,' said Arthur flatly. 'I haven't seen him all summer.'

'But didn't you tell him you're not allowed to see him either?'

'I couldn't,' said Arthur. 'After Christmas, after Papa said, well, it was holidays. I just never saw him again. I couldn't tell him if I never saw him could I.'

'Well, obviously his father doesn't like this occupation thing,' said Ida. 'Doesn't want his boy mixing with no dirty Kiwilander kid.'

Arthur was shocked. 'Is that what he said?'

'Of course not,' said his grandmother. 'They never say that out loud, boy. But that's what they think, isn't it.'

'I don't know,' said a dejected Arthur. 'Did he say anything else?'

'Just sorry, boy. He said sorry.'

'I'm sorry too,' said Arthur.

'I know, boy,' said Ida kindly. 'I told him that. Told him you'd be just as sorry as him.'

Arthur smiled wanly. 'Thanks, Grandmama,' he said.

*

Before long it was clear to Cyril, Alfred, and the other supporting councillors, that there was a hardcore of three to four hundred men and women prepared to spend every day and night in the camp. They were the heart of the occupation. But Cyril also discovered that word of the protest had spread to Kiwilanders throughout the country. He learned that people were coming to the village on the expensive V-1 Rapid Brynderwyn Tunnel service from Wellington and Auckland as well as on the V-2 Stopping service from all the other southern districts, to lend at least moral support. They came and went in waves, mostly at weekends, working around their own domestic and work commitments. They came to give their time and whatever support they could in the form of their knowledge, expertise, skill, and physical labour, doing whatever was asked of them. They also brought food, tents and bedding as well as miscellaneous building materials they thought might be useful.

Whoever they were, wherever they came from, whatever they brought and whatever they did, their comings and goings, and all the outdoor activities of the camp, were seen and recorded by the hiding Peace Officers whose observations were eventually passed on to the government. It was for this reason that a lot of people, villagers and backlanders, who otherwise supported the occupation in principle, were reluctant — too timid, too confused, too colonized, basically too afraid — to give the protest their overt support; they simply didn't want their names to be on the government's record.

Before long the Flitcroft Point plateau came to resemble the nascent Flitcroft village of 2076. Indeed, without realizing it, Cyril Flitcroft had acted as a surveyor and town planner just as his great-grandfather, Henri, had a hundred and one years earlier. As more people arrived to stay he directed them to set up their tents in orderly rows. And the unpromising-looking building materials which supporters brought — wood, bricks, roofing, windows and doors, drainage tiles and more — were somehow, under his supervision, assembled into reasonably weatherproof huts.

Inspired by his leadership, suitably qualified tradesmen contrived to pump, pipe and store water from a standpipe in the church cemetery while locals and newcomers combined to erect cold-water showers and latrines on the northern side, sloping away from the camp plateau. Meanwhile, experienced and clever gardeners from the backlands established, maintained and cropped extensive vegetable gardens on the Point's sunny lower slopes. Poultry farmers brought in lightweight movable fencing and nesting boxes to contain laying hens which provided fresh eggs to the kitchen which the village women had established and in which they shared the work of preparing and serving generous and nutritious meals to anyone who needed them.

Other less-desirable supporters came with their own agendas, Kiwilanders and Vandiers both, with political opinions based in the extremes of left and right. They brought their grudges against the government, hoping to advance their particular campaign by associating them with what was obviously getting more attention from the public and the government than their own various and petty causes. Whoever they were, whatever their cause and motivation, they were made welcome by Cyril and the councillors providing only that they contributed to the smooth running of the camp and the occupation.

14

DESPITE THE SUPPORT — from outsiders and more than a few Vandiers — there was some disharmony, some disagreement and unpleasantness, concerning camp management. When the occupation was proposed, at the village meeting, not all the village councillors, sitting together on the stage in apparent solidarity, agreed with the idea, despite it being overwhelmingly adopted by the meeting. After all, they said, Cyril Flitcroft was just one councillor, not even the chairman, and he had no authority to propose let alone lead such a protest.

Oscar Bladen, the newly-elected chairman of the village council, to whom the government notice had been served and who had been so shocked by the government's blatant disregard of both history and tradition, had supported Cyril from the beginning, as had Cyril's friend, Walter Turpin. Of the others — Hugh Wombourne, the immediate past chairman, Primus Townend, Yaxley Heath and Wilfred Cranleigh — Heath and Cranleigh disagreed with the protest and occupation, each for reasons connected with his business's dependence on Vandier customers, and, over the next few months, worked actively to undermine the protesters' solidarity and morale. As a result, Cyril and the other supporting councillors, together with Cyril's father, Alfred, and Hugh Wombourne's wife, Doreen, recruited a few other staunch men and women to form what they called an Action Committee.

Chief among the recruits were Stanley Buckley-Young, a wealthy young backlands poultry farmer who had plenty of staff to cope in his absence, Benedict Hudnut who had a second-hand and pawn shop in the village, and Beatrice Heveningham, a brilliant young professor of Kiwiland history from Wellington University who had left her university post to support the occupation on historic principle.

It was this committee which thereafter organized the running of the camp, led the protest, and represented the Kiwilanders' cause in the government negotiations which had begun, albeit tentatively.

In one of many gestures meant to be conciliatory, the government offered to sell back part of the Point land and so return it to village ownership. The offer came via a condescending petty official sent to the Point for the purpose. He came alone, had no idea to whom the offer should be made, and had to be directed to Cyril Flitcroft who then called the Action Committee together to hear what the evidently official but obviously nervous and powerless visitor had to say. However, the portion of land offered was so small and undesirable, and the asking price so large, that Cyril and the Action Committee considered the offer as no better than an insult.

'To pay that much money to buy back just a small bit of our own land is ridiculous,' Cyril said to the puzzled envoy in English (meaning that to be an insult) before repeating his response in Vandient.

As time passed the government made other offers but it seemed to the Action Committee that none was made seriously. They appeared to be merely theatrical gestures designed to test the Kiwilanders' resolve as the government waited for winter when it expected the protest to collapse.

Eviction was threatened occasionally, by various government representatives of various ranks, including, once, by the Superior of the Peace Force, but no action ever followed.

However, as each offer was received it was always reported to the camp meeting.

At first, during the warm summer evenings, the camp meetings were informal affairs, held outside every second night or so, with everyone sitting around on the grass. But as autumn advanced the meetings moved into the big, all-purpose marquee. Cyril and the others realized, though, that if the evening meetings were to continue they would need better shelter from the cold wind, rain and storms of winter to which Flitcroft Point, projecting out into the sea, was more exposed than the village and backlands.

After a discussion on the matter, in the middle of April, as the days grew short and temperatures cooled, a villager working on a building site in

Whangārei convinced his sympathetic Vandier employer to allow him and a few protester friends to dismantle a large hall which was destined for demolition to make way for something bigger and grander. The work was completed over one weekend. They then transported the parts to Flitcroft Point where they were reassembled in the approximate middle of the camp. It was a simple building, formerly used by the True and Loyal Band of Brothers, a semi-religious Vandier fraternity, but it served the camp perfectly well as a Great Hall, an all-weather replacement for the marquee used for communal dining, parties and social events, as well as the venue for the important evening meetings throughout that winter.

*

Meanwhile the Action Committee continued to welcome any support, whatever its form.

Most welcome were those who joined the occupation more or less permanently and were not only self-sufficient and self-reliant but also brought a useful trade or skill or willingly provided their labour wherever and whenever it was required. Apart from the trades connected with building and construction, and the backlanders who brought their chickens, and knew how to raise vegetable gardens, other professionals unexpectedly brought knowledge and skills to satisfy needs which Cyril had never anticipated.

Hugh Wombourne of the Action Committee, who was the village barber and immediate past chairman of the village council, set aside one day a fortnight to cut the hair of camp men (and their sons) without charge. His wife, Doreen, a hairdresser and beautician who was also on the Action Committee, provided the same service for women and girls.

It was one thing to have a plentiful supply of food — including donations, meat from the farms and fresh vegetables from the camp's gardens — but it required the service of professional butchers to prepare the meat, and the experience of cooks and chefs to organize and run a big kitchen and prepare and serve sometimes hundreds of meals with maximum efficiency and minimum waste.

In the beginning Cyril never imagined that the Action Committee would need a proper office. But it did. Agendas, minutes, newsletters, posters, flyers and more needed to be printed, copied and distributed. Filing systems needed to be organized and maintained. Enquiries from foreign governments, news organizations, and other oppressed and protesting minority groups from around the world, needed to be answered. And so, from somewhere, somehow, young men and women — bookkeepers, clerks, programmers, writers, artists, journalists, photographers — trained and experienced, appeared, as if from nowhere, to organize an office the size and efficiency of which always amazed Cyril.

Indeed, it seemed that whenever a special skill or talent was required, people willing and ideally qualified presented themselves for service. Where they came from, how it happened, was a mystery that Cyril never solved but came to accept as a heavenly gift.

15

THERE WERE CASUAL visitors too, Kiwilanders *and* Vandiers. The curious were indulged — offered hospitality and allowed to stay a few nights if they wished — but discouraged from hanging around the site watching others work. Cyril and the Action Committee believed that by mixing with the campers, and especially by attending at least one or two of the meetings in the Great Hall, those folk evidently just passing through out of curiosity would learn of the historic injustices imposed on Kiwilanders by successive governments and so understand the purpose and legitimacy of the occupation. It was hoped, not unreasonably, that when they returned to their normal lives such curious visitors would act as ambassadors for a cause which by then they understood.

A few, though, coming first from idle curiosity — perhaps unemployed or between seasonal jobs — stayed from choice and contributed much.

One important category of daytime visitors arrived with a genuine interest in the occupation's cause. They came from both Kiwilander and Vandier societies and were usually recognized as important figures in some way. The Action Committee came to call them V.I.P.s. They showed their sympathy and support not with their skills or labour but with generous donations of cash, as well as promises to promote the Flitcroft Point cause however and whenever they could in whatever their field of influence. Due to their eminence, and the demands on their time, they were rarely able to visit for more than a few hours. Despite the brevity of their visits, their individual and collective importance and influence made their support valuable and valued. As a result, whether they were Kiwilander or Vandier, they were always treated with respect and introduced at the Great Hall evening meetings with appropriate deference.

It was at those evening meetings in the Great Hall that many visitors heard for the first time the full and true extent of the government's historic exploitation of the Kiwilanders and their land. They learned in detail what until then they had known only as unsettling rumours; matters of history that had been forgotten or intentionally suppressed by the government.

For example they learned, from Cyril and others of the Action Committee, or from anyone who had something to report which they had once learned from their parents or grandparents, about how in former times children were forbidden to speak English at school or in the company of Vandiers.

'The government always despised our culture and language,' said one man, old but not as old as Enoch Flitcroft. 'They thought we needed to speak Vandient and act more like Vandiers if we wanted to be happy.'

They learned how, in 2107, the remaining priests of the Kiwilanders' religion were forbidden to practice or preach or promote Christian festivals or conduct the traditional Christian rituals connected with birth, marriage and death.

'My poor father, Henri — a priest of our religion — died that year,' said old Enoch, 'of a broken heart.'

That surprised many listeners; the government's suppression of priests was unknown by most people and forgotten by the rest.

'That's why I do my best to stand in for my father in our little church,' explained the old man.

They heard — many for the first time — how the government had long ago taken Flitcroft Point as a defensive measure against an expected invasion that never came, promising to return it when the threat was over. It was, of course, never returned.

And then they were reminded how, only twenty-five years earlier, the government had evicted those few village residents remaining on Flitcroft Point and then failed in their promise to replace their demolished houses.

'You know why they demolished those houses, don't you,' said Enoch, and it wasn't a question. 'Because the President of the Republic was paying a visit and they thought our houses were too unsightly for his delicate eyes.'

'I remember that,' shouted Edmund Healy, whose family was one of those evicted from their home on the heights of Flitcroft Point. 'What's more, after we were evicted the Great Hall there burned down in a mysterious and suspicious fire.'

'Because of the President's visit,' said Enoch with disgust.

'That was when we built the new Great Hall on our farm,' said Alfred Flitcroft, who stood up then. 'Bugger them, we thought,' he added angrily. 'They can't touch us there. Not on our own land.'

'I wouldn't count on it,' called a sceptical voice from the audience.

*

There were always some casual visitors — not many — who arrived with nothing on their mind but mischief. In the beginning they were usually harmless, more of a nuisance than a threat, and were tolerated for a while before being politely asked to leave; a request which was usually followed by good-natured compliance. But as the months passed, and winter set in — when the nights were long — the campers reported many more casual visitors coming freely onto the site apparently looking for trouble. The Action Committee didn't know whether they were simply idle troublesome types or had been intentionally recruited by opponents of the occupation hoping to provoke a physical response that would undermine the protest's non-violent strategy. They suspected the latter.

In the interests of the safety of all campers, especially vulnerable women and children sleeping in makeshift shelters, the Action Committee decided that unfortunately, and contrary to its policy of openness and cordial hospitality, it would have to take three security measures.

Firstly, a tall wooden tower was built near the centre of the camp from the very top of which observers rostered throughout the daylight hours could see the entire surrounding camp and beyond, including up to the bushline, down to the beach, the cemetery and church, and up the full length of Beach Street to the village.

Secondly, a high fence was erected along the length of the Beach Street boundary; it had a wide double gate through which all visitors would have to pass.

Thirdly, the gate was manned by a cadre of watchmen chosen from volunteers partly for their youth but also for their willingness to sometimes sacrifice a full night's sleep in order to patrol the camp at night. Some dog owners also volunteered. While admitting that their dogs were beloved pets, untrained for guard duty — 'If my Kaiser finds an intruder he's more likely to lick him to death,' said one owner — it was generally agreed that a dog's superior senses, especially at night, were invaluable, and that the presence, growl and bark of even a small dog would intimidate any hostile prowler.

16

WITH THE COMING of winter the campers knew from experience what to expect; or *thought* they knew. But knowing from experience how wet, cold, windy and miserable winter could be, when the experience came from the shelter of home, office or factory, was not *really* knowing. And even those who normally had to work in the open air, in all weathers, were usually able to spend the wet, cold, windy and stormy nights of winter firstly in front of a homely fire and then in a warm bed sheltered by solid walls, weatherproof doors and windows, and a watertight roof.

Nothing could have prepared anyone for the harsh reality of living, day and night, in impermanent accommodation, on a high and exposed promontory on the east coast of Northland for an entire winter. Those in tents suffered the most, but even those sleeping in huts and sheds discovered that the jerry-built nature of their accommodation was not enough to keep out the cold, howling winds and driving rain of a typical winter.

The lush green pasture of the Point's plateau, so pleasant to stroll over on fine summer days, and so soft to sit upon on balmy evenings, listening to talks, or enchanting music from resident or visiting singers and musicians, quickly lost its romantic charm when rain turned it cold, wet and slippery, and hundreds of booted feet churned it into cold mud, black and cloying. Every walk, day or night — to the showers or latrines, Great Hall or kitchen, to a neighbour's tent or hut, or back to Beach Road and the village — became a heavy gumbooted slog made worse if it were raining, even worse if the rain was driven by a fierce wind to sting the cold and numbing face and hands.

*

One Saturday afternoon in the middle of August, a day that was surprisingly fine and mild — although not fine and mild enough for long enough to dry out the sticky bog that was the campsite — Cyril received a message from the gate. He was sitting with Alfred, Ida and Arthur on camp chairs outside the hut which had become the Flitcroft home. The sky was clear, the sea smooth, and they were looking out to sea, watching a long parade of ships moving silently south heading for the Whangārei shipping port. They were thoroughly relaxed, having shared a communal lunch in the Great Hall, enjoying the fine weather, when one of the young guards arrived and excused himself to announce that there was a strange visitor at the gate wanting to see Mr Flitcroft.

'What's so strange about him?' asked Cyril.

'It's amazing, man,' said the youth, whose name was Connor.

'What is?'

'He's only a kid,' said Connor.

'A kid?'

'A boy. About the age of young Arthur there.'

'So?'

'He's a Vandier kid, Mr Flitcroft,' said Connor. 'And he speaks perfect English. If you closed your eyes...'

Arthur stood up at once. 'It must be Mot-L,' he said. 'It *must* be, Papa. Must be.'

Cyril didn't comment on Arthur's excitement. Nor did he show any surprise at Connor's news. He merely looked up and asked, 'What does he want?'

'Wouldn't say,' said Connor. 'Just wants to see you. Mr Flitcroft, he said. In English. Perfect English.'

'Well then, I suppose you better bring him up and we'll hear what he has to say.'

What Mot-L had to say — in perfect English — was that he had been sent by his father, the Superior of the Peace Force...

'I know who your father is, boy,' interrupted Cyril, rather rudely thought Arthur. He and Mot-L had already exchanged friendly nods of acknowledgement.

'I'm sorry,' said Mot-L. 'Of course you do. Well,' he continued, 'I'm to say that I'm here in a completely unofficial capacity you understand...'

'Because you can speak English,' interrupted Cyril again. And again Arthur thought his father was being rude.

'Yes. My father thought...'

'I can see what your father thought,' said Cyril gruffly, but Mot-L was not put off.

'Well, he said to say that the government has been patient so far and that as the worst of winter is still to come it might be better for everyone if you all went home and forgot about this protest and that if you do everything will return to normal and there will be no repercussions or unpleasantness,' said the visiting boy in a breathless unbroken stream.

'That's a pretty long speech,' said Cyril.

'I had to translate it and memorize it in English,' said Mot-L. 'I hope it was right. I hope you understood.'

'I understood perfectly well, boy,' said Cyril who was impressed with the young herald's confidence, courtesy and bearing as much as he was with his English competency.

'Am I to take back a reply?' asked Mot-L.

Cyril looked around; at Arthur, at his mother and father. Only his mother spoke.

'The Action Committee?' she asked.

Cyril shook his head. 'No need,' he said. 'We're all resolved.'

Ida nodded, understanding.

Cyril turned to the standing and waiting young Vandier.

'I'm impressed with your English, boy,' he said.

'His name's Mot-L,' said Arthur.

'Mot-L,' repeated Cyril awkwardly and with a distinct Kiwilander accent. 'But you can tell your father, well, thank him first, properly, from the

Flitcroft Point Action Committee. Say that. Understand?

'Yes, sir.'

'Good. And then tell him that we're not moving. We'll be here for as long as it takes. Do you understand?'

'Not really,' said Mot-L. 'I understand the words. But what do you mean? As long as it takes. I don't understand.'

'Your father'll understand, boy,' said Cyril.

'I'll tell him. What you said,' said Mot-L. 'I'll tell him exactly. You're not moving. You'll be here for as long as it takes.'

'Not from me, you understand? Say it's from the Action Committee.'

'The Action Committee,' repeated Mot-L.

'That's it, boy,' said Cyril. 'Exactly. And thank you.' And then, still somewhat impressed by the boy's confident but courteous attitude, he added, 'Now I know you and Arthur are pals, so why don't you stop here with him for a while.'

It was something both boys were glad to hear.

Cyril had guessed that. 'Will that be all right with your father?' he asked.

'I think so, sir, yes,' said Mot-L. 'Thank you.'

'You can have dinner with us later,' continued Cyril with a friendliness which surprised but pleased Arthur. 'With everybody.' And then, because he saw the presence of this intelligent English-speaking Vandier boy as an opportunity, he added, 'And because you understand English so well, you can come to tonight's meeting. You might find it interesting. Would you like that?'

'Oh, yes,' said Mot-L who enjoyed speaking English with a native speaker — an adult — and was thrilled to be surrounded and tested by people speaking only English. He was glad he understood everything that was said and that everything he said was understood.

'You'll probably hear Arthur's great-grandfather speak,' said Cyril. 'He's a hundred and six years old.'

'I've heard of him,' said Mot-L. 'He's famous. The oldest man in the country.'

'Yes,' said Cyril. 'The oldest man in the country.'

And, he thought but didn't say, the only person now alive who remembers the coming of your people, the Vandiers.

The only one.

17

ARTHUR SPENT THAT fine but cold afternoon showing Mot-L around the camp. He learned, as they walked together up and down the site's muddy tracks, around the camp perimeter, how little his friend knew about ordinary Kiwilanders, the history of Flitcroft village and, especially, the short- and long-term grievances which led to the protesting occupation of Flitcroft Point.

'So what do they want, your people?' asked Mot-L.

'They want all this back,' said Arthur. 'Flitcroft Point. They gave it to the government in the olden days, sort of lent it for a while, but the government kept it and is now going to build houses there which Kiwilanders would never be able to afford. And then they're going to stop ordinary people from going there for picnics and stuff like that.'

'Is that what your father means when he says your people will stay for as long as it takes?'

'Yes,' said Arthur.

'Until the government gives back all of Flitcroft Point? For picnics and things?'

'Yes,' said Arthur, to which Mot-L nodded slowly and sagely in understanding, more like an old man than a young boy.

Now, having spent the afternoon together, and then joining the communal dinner, the two boys were sitting cross-legged on the floor of the Great Hall, directly in front of the low stage, with a few of Arthur's other friends from school, including Doral Turpin. And there, for the next hour or so, the children looked up and listened to the night's speakers.

The talks were all given and received seriously but without rancour. Arthur was relieved that the target was always the arrogant and deceitful government; that no anger was directed at the Vandier people. All the same, he was somewhat embarrassed for Mot-L who seemed to be listening with rapt attention to every English word from every speaker. But despite his discomfort Arthur hoped that his friend might come to understand what it was like to be a minority in your own country; to be outnumbered many times by people who, through an accident of history, had all the power, all the money. Mot-L didn't acknowledge any such thing — he didn't say *anything* about what he had heard that night — but Arthur sensed that his friend had learned a lot from the night's speakers.

The Great Hall fell quiet when Enoch began to speak.

Many of the people in the audience had heard most of his stories before but on this occasion his address was especially affecting. Everyone was gripped by the old man's extraordinary charisma and the knowledge and authority he conveyed, not only in his simple words but in the dignified manner in which they were so quietly but convincingly delivered.

He began by telling his audience, briefly, of a series of past events, examples of the contempt with which the government had treated the Kiwilanders for more than a hundred years, which had led to the present protest on Flitcroft Point.

Then, to the audience's surprise, he moved to an affair of which few of them had ever heard. He told how, in 2078, when he was just seven years old, the Kiwilanders of that time had granted the entire but somewhat run down city of Whangārei — twelve hundred hectares on the edge of Whangārei harbour — to the new government, as a gesture of goodwill, on the understanding that it would develop a new, modern city to serve *all* the people of Northland, Kiwilanders and Vandiers. Furthermore it was agreed that all unused land would be set aside as public space, landscaped with trees, gardens, footpaths and ponds, for the free use of all people in perpetuity.

A nominal payment — a token gesture — was agreed and paid.

But then came the scandal which the Kiwilanders then had so resented and would have been forgotten now if not for Enoch Flitcroft: only one year later the government broke up the land into many lots which were sold to private developers, without reference to the former owners, for more than two hundred and thirty times what it had paid the naïve Kiwilanders.

'That,' said the speaker, 'is the land which was once ours. Priceless land that's now the heart of modern Whangārei. And it's all privately owned by Vandiers.'

The old man paused then for effect before adding in conclusion, 'And if that's not theft, I don't know what is.'

The audience members — especially the many visitors, Kiwilander and Vandier, including Arthur's friend, Mot-L — were shocked by Enoch's tale of government greed and deceit. They saw, more clearly than ever, that the recent enforced taking of the Flitcroft Beach land was only the latest in a long and connected series of events in which successive governments had taken advantage of successive generations of naïve and trusting Kiwilanders.

'But we're naïve and trusting no more,' insisted Cyril Flitcroft at the end of each meeting. 'The exploitation everywhere stops right here. On Flitcroft Point. Now.'

*

Old Enoch didn't get up the next morning. He said he was exhausted by the previous night's meeting, which had been physically and emotionally draining.

It was Sunday.

'You stay there, Papa Enoch,' said Ida. 'Cyril will go to church for you. He knows what to say. What to do.'

The old man managed to nod his head in understanding, resignation and thanks.

'The people will come from the Point to pray for you, Papa Enoch.'

The old man nodded again. But his eyes were closed. Ida stood looking down at him. She thought he looked tiny. His thin and bony arms were crossed on top of the covers so she felt his hands; they were cold. His breathing was fast and shallow. She knew the signs. The old man was leaving after a hundred and six remarkable years.

Enoch Flitcroft died peacefully in his sleep in the early hours of the next morning, his daughter-in-law at his bedside. His funeral was held the next evening, and once again his young and strong grandson, Cyril, chose to dig the grave himself beside the one in which he had buried his young wife only a little more than fifteen months since. And it was he, Cyril Flitcroft the gravedigger, who also conducted the funeral service, reading from the Book of Common Prayer which had been presented to his great-grandfather, Enoch's father, Henri Flitcroft, to mark his ordination in 2071, the year of now-dead Enoch's birth.

Only when he was back on the Point after the funeral did Cyril have time to consider the implications of his grandfather's passing. Surely, he thought, the government would be glad to learn of the death of Enoch Henri Flitcroft.

He was right.

The government knew that Enoch Flitcroft was the country's last survivor of his generation. It knew that only he could remember the conquest which occurred, after the passing of the sicknesses, more than a hundred years ago. It knew that his living mind was a repository of unpleasant memories which conflicted with the government's official history and so made him a threat to its authority and the nation's race relations.

Indeed, Enoch's knowledge and memories — of the Kiwilanders and their history — were so great that many people who may once have been indifferent to their origins, if not actually ashamed of their race and ancestry, came away from his talks uplifted and proud. They were — and said to him that they were — immensely grateful to him who had suffered so much and yet managed to retain pride in his culture, his race, his religion and his language.

It was a contagious pride which, through his talks in the Great Hall, he successfully transferred to so many people.

That was to be his greatest legacy.

18

THE WINTER OF 2177 was a test which many of the protesters at least partly failed. A hard core remained, stubbornly steadfast — acting more on principle than anything else — and it was only due to their fortitude that the occupation was not abandoned.

The demands on farmers and backlanders to return regularly to their land were lower in the winter which meant they could stay for longer periods. But even they, accustomed to working outside but retreating at night to the warmth and security of their homes, were tested by winter on the exposed Point while living in a tent, caravan or draughty and leaky hut. Many others softened their protest to some extent, although more from necessity than weakness, especially when pressured by unsympathetic or impatient families, employers or colleagues. Those who really couldn't manage the winter nights reluctantly returned home at the end of each day. Some, the most vulnerable, left for the winter duration. They included the old, a few mothers-to-be, and mothers with infants and toddlers, worried about their children's health.

However, all who left the camp — for whatever reason and for however long — promised to return in the spring. And all did, without exception. But before then, as winter turned to spring, the protesters — whether braving the last of the winter weather on the Point or sheltering at home, whether man or woman, boy or girl, whether young or old, Kiwilander or Vandier — all had to endure and share an unspeakable tragedy.

*

Late one night at the end of September 2177, as the Action Committee and a few others were gathered in the Great Hall, discussing a rumour that two former but hostile village councillors were working to take advantage of the campers' low winter morale, a woman's dreadful scream — and another and another and yet another — sliced thinly through the chill air, like sharp and jagged lightning, to race into the Great Hall and instantly strike dead the meeting.

The men and women there looked at each other in alarm, for a second or two, before running together through the night, along slushy and muddy pathways, towards the sound of the screams, which stopped only long enough for the screamer to take another breath. It was the most awful sound any of them had ever heard: the sound of a woman shrieking with the unbearable pain of a torn heart.

They, the running members of the Action Committee, stopped, horrified, when they found Kelpie Turpin kneeling in the mud, cradling the limp and lifeless body of her eldest son, Doral.

The hut in which the boy had been sleeping was a mess of wet, stinking, blackened wood, burnt but still smouldering with ghostly wisps of smoke, glowing pink and ashy grey. Three of the night's watchmen stood helplessly beside the smoky ruins while another, Murray Ambrose, kneeled helplessly at the side of the now bent and sobbing Kelpie, his dog, Atilla, sitting, panting, at his back.

Others arrived, most wearing pyjamas and dressing gowns, some in bare feet, and they formed a circle around the scene; a circle of white faces and wide, white eyes staring down with shock at the unbelievably sad and pathetic scene. Many of the women, and some of the men, too, sobbed uncontrollably. Small children stared uncomprehendingly from behind their parents, to whose legs they clung as if for protection.

It was the watchmen with their dogs who had first smelled the smoke and then found the fire. While one of them had fetched Kelpie, the others had put out the fire, easily enough, with buckets of water. They found Doral lying inside the ruins. But they were too late. He was unharmed by the flames — they had saved him from that — but he had died from breathing the smoke. Now he lay outside, pale and limp, in the arms of his sobbing and unbelieving mother, his pyjamas, his white face, and the uncovered parts of his arms and legs, smudged with black.

Kelpie stopped screaming when people arrived. Now, still sobbing uncontrollably, she lifted her dead son's head, its face damp and dirty with smuts, pushed back his long brown bangs, and kissed him again and again and again and again and again.

'Oh, God, my darling Doral,' she cried repeatedly between kisses. 'My dearest darling boy. What have they done to you? What have they done?'

Cradling the innocent one's head, she looked up at the circle of people as if searching for someone. At last she saw her husband standing, stunned and speechless, as if his feet were stuck in the cold mud.

'Walter Turpin,' she screamed. 'What have you done to our boy?'

At that, Walter fell to her side, kneeling in the mud, sobbing, as he stroked the dead child's soft but cold and black-smudged cheek.

The circle of campers, standing helplessly, either numb with shock or sobbing and weeping, seemed to have no idea what to do next. The sound of sirens then came up the hill from Beach Street.

'And you, too, Cyril Flitcroft,' howled the almost hysterical woman, looking about blindly, helplessly, hopelessly, 'wherever the hell you are. Murderer. You're all of you murderers.'

'Kelpie. Please,' begged Walter. But she pushed him away and shouted, 'Leave me alone, you bastard.'

And then, looking up and around at the crowd again, she shrieked, 'You're all bastards! Murdering bastards!' before collapsing, sobbing, over the body of her precious but dead son, Doral, who had just reached his twelfth birthday.

'That'll be the fire brigade and the ambulance,' said Murray Ambrose to Cyril.

'Bit late now,' said Cyril grimly.

Despite tradition, Walter Turpin couldn't bring himself to dig Doral's grave. He didn't know why, couldn't explain it, couldn't even begin to explain it, but he just couldn't. Indeed, he could hardly do anything. Estranged from his wife, he was numb.

Nothing was said by the other men of the Action Committee. They knew things might have been said — *should* have been said — to Walter as well as to each other. But, being men of action, they didn't know what those things might be and even if they did they wouldn't know where to find the words to express them. The women of the camp, though, including the two activist women on the Action Committee, knew exactly what to say and do and continued to both understand and comfort Kelpie in her loud and obvious grief and, separately, comfort Walter in his own silent suffering.

In the end it was Cyril Flitcroft who dug the small grave, the latest in a line after his young wife and old grandfather. But it was Oscar Bladen the undertaker — not Cyril — who conducted the funeral service.

It was the end of day. The sun was falling in the western sky and although it was spring the air was chilled by a swirling wind coming off the sea. Walter and Kelpie Turpin stood together with their children, Kelpie holding little Kenneth, wriggling with impatience and disinterest, the other children looking pale and shocked. They were together at one end of the grave while Oscar stood alone at the other. Despite the use of a Tannoy, Oscar's words of prayer were often blown away by the wind and so were barely heard by the vast crowd. The group of both Kiwilanders and Vandiers overflowed the small cemetery, spilling down onto the beach and across into the beach-side strip of land so recently appropriated by the government which action was the very cause of the Flitcroft Point occupation.

19

KELPIE TURPIN NEVER recovered from Doral's death. She never returned to the occupation and came to hate its very existence.

At first Walter Turpin stayed reluctantly on the Point, stayed with Cyril and the others on the Action Committee, only because he wasn't welcome at home. Before long, however, he did quit the Action Committee, the protest and the occupation, and returned home to be with his inconsolable wife. She was, and remained, a broken woman. Life for them had become a shared misery.

Doral's tragic death also affected the mood of the occupation. It seemed to hang like a pall over the whole camp as if the smoke which had killed him had never dispersed.

But summer came at last. The grass recovered, although what was once a smooth carpet of green pasture had become broken and lumpy; the stirred-up impressions made by a winter's worth of tramping booted feet were hardened into permanence by the summer sun.

The return of fine and warm weather marked the return of most of the campers and protesters who had reluctantly surrendered to the winter cold, rain and gales. But while Cyril and the remaining members of the Action Committee appeared as committed as ever to the occupation, many of the returning and supporting protesters realized, on quietly analysing their motives, that their commitment now was partly in memory of Doral Turpin. They felt that if their protest failed then the poor boy's life would have been lost in vain.

As the year drew to an end the government began sending more and more-senior officials with a series of offers that were never enough and would never be enough. The Action Committee was resolved to accept nothing less than the full return of all the Flitcroft Point land including the beachfront strip so recently appropriated.

Money of any amount, they insisted, was not the issue.

*

It was nearly Christmas before Arthur returned to the Point.

Ida had stayed home after Enoch's funeral and Arthur had joined her after Doral's, not even staying with his father on weekends. Having experienced the death and funerals of his mother, whom he loved dearly, (and his stillborn baby brother, whom he never saw), and his great-grandfather, whom he respected greatly rather than loved, the awful death of his friend, Doral, shocked him dreadfully.

He had seen his dead mother and grandfather only after they had been prepared for burial by Mr and Mrs Bladen, but he was haunted by what he saw that night, on Flitcroft Point, beside the glowing and smoking embers and mess of Doral's hut: his dead friend, lying limp and unbreathing in his mother's arms, as cold as the ground on which he lay, his long, brown hair lying wet and stringy across his forehead; his white almost transparent skin fouled by dirty black smudges.

When at last he returned to the Point, to the hut which his father and grandfather were still using, his busy and preoccupied father didn't say much. He did tousle his head rather roughly and said only, almost in passing, 'Summer's here, boy. School will be finished soon.'

Arthur merely nodded, thinking only how much he now missed going to and from school with Doral.

He was glad, though, when one day after school Mot-L came to the house, without warning.

'I'm sorry I haven't seen you for so long,' said the Vandier boy in English. 'My father thought it was better to stay away, you know.'

'I know,' said Arthur.

'It must have been awful.'

'It was,' said Arthur, after which they never again spoke of Doral Turpin and the fire.

'My father says the government is getting really impatient now,' said Mot-L.

'My father has guessed the same,' said Arthur.

'It's stalemate, isn't it,' said Mot-L to which Arthur nodded grimly.

The boys then resumed their long-abandoned habit of meeting most days after school. They discovered, though, that there was no need for secrecy. It seemed that their fathers had each decided — without reference to the other — that it was not a bad thing for their sons to meet.

On fine days they met in the occupation camp where they spoke only English. Unlike Arthur, who heard Vandient spoken wherever he went, Mot-L was surrounded by English speakers only when on the Point.

'It's really good when I have to speak English all the time,' he said. 'No one in my family, no one I even know, can speak it at all. Just a few common words, that's all. And they mostly get them wrong anyway.'

On less fine days they met in Ida's garden shed where they played and discussed chess and spoke only in Vandient. They were now more evenly-matched players which meant that many if not most games ended in a draw.

'I can beat my father most times now,' said Mot-L at the end of a drawn game with Arthur. 'Thanks to you.'

Arthur admitted that he, too, was now a better player.

'Thanks to my Great-Grandpapa's old book, really,' said Arthur, pointing to the ancient Bobby Fischer book which he now kept in a wooden box as it was falling apart from overuse. It was, after all, more than two hundred years old, and very delicate, so they now referred to it only occasionally.

*

Christmas day, 2177, a Thursday, arrived without fanfare, progressed as any other day, and ended rather flatly.

As usual, the village Kiwilanders preferred to minimise any show of religion knowing that Vandiers had no respect for their religious beliefs. And so they waited until the end of the day — when school and businesses were closed — to meet in their little church to observe the birth of the founder of their religion, Jesus Christ, to whom, and to God his father, they prayed.

But the service was poorly attended. Not only did the death of Doral Turpin still haunt the whole populace — in the camp as well as in the village, including those not supporting the occupation — but there was a feeling abroad that the Flitcroft Point protest was going on too long, without any signs of success, and that the activist protest leader, Cyril Flitcroft, so determined, so persuasive, and sometimes so fiery in his exhortations, was not the right person this Christmas to read from the ancient and precious books he had inherited from his grandfather, Enoch.

The following week's New Year's Eve celebration was similarly muted. The idea of the traditional bonfire was discarded unanimously, without debate, for obvious reasons. Then, without a bonfire, there seemed no point in having fireworks and so the focus of the celebration was lost.

Many people drifted away even before that midnight hour arrived; the small crowd remaining was easily accommodated in the big marquee, open-sided for the occasion in recognition of the night's warmth and humidity.

It was there, in that marquee, that the men of the village usually gathered on New Year's Eve to celebrate the occasion with the excessive consumption of the village's strong ale. That no ale or any strong drink was consumed that night, in the big marquee or anywhere, was not the only reason for the party's sober character.

There was singing, of course, "Auld Lang Syne" being bravely rendered as the year ended. But as the singing faded away and the crowd thinned, and as the year 2178 began, Cyril Flitcroft sat quietly at a table outside the marquee, with his father and a few of the men of the Action Committee, dreaming perhaps of years past and ale-pots emptied, and reminiscing about the year gone and speculating about that which lay ahead.

'It was this night a year ago,' said Cyril, meaning the night of January the first, 2177, 'that me and my father here,' at which he pointed across the table to Alfred, 'went up to the bushline, up there on the Point, and found the lines on the grass. Isn't that right, Papa?'

'Bloody right,' said Alfred, ignoring the fact that it was Kelpie Turpin who had discovered the lines

— leading to her arrest by the Peace Force — and Arthur and Doral who had reported them on New Year's Day. 'But they're gone now,' he added. 'Bloody washed away.'

'And a good thing too,' said Cyril.

'And then tomorrow, a year tomorrow don't forget,' continued Cyril, remembering, talking almost to himself, and then looking at Oscar Bladen, 'they came to take away our beach land.'

Oscar Bladen nodded heavily.

'The last straw,' said Cyril.

'Bastards,' said his father.

Cyril raised a clenched fist as if he were holding a heavy mug of ale.

'Happy New Year,' he said.

And his companions all raised their clenched fists, holding their invisible pots together over the centre of the table.

'Happy new year,' they said together. 'Happy new year.'

20

UNFORTUNATELY THE YEAR which followed was far from happy.

It's true that the camp was back to full strength all that summer, and the mood of the campers was cheerful and optimistic.

The routines so firmly established during the first summer, which were somewhat disrupted by the hardships of winter and the reduced population, were quickly restored. Once again people found ways to balance their support of the occupation with the demands of their home duties, their children, their job, business, or farm. And, to the huge relief of the Action Committee, who feared that support might have waned over winter, encouragement and help continued to be received from Kiwilander communities and sympathetic (and sometimes wealthy) Vandiers throughout the country.

Mot-L spent some of almost every day of the summer holidays with Arthur. At first they played apart from the other children, exploring the beach and the rocks around the base of the Point. It was all familiar territory to Arthur who had been taken to the beach by his mother since he was a toddler. It was there, too, that many of the village women spent the hours of low tide probing and grasping into the sand for fat and healthy shellfish which they turned into delicious and nutritious chowders.

Before long Arthur introduced Mot-L to his friends in the camp. The Vandier boy found he was immediately accepted into the circle of Kiwilander boys and girls his own age and that the games they played were pretty much the same as the games he played with his Vandier friends at school; only the language used was different. Thus, the hours and days spent with Arthur and his friends added a convincing polish to his spoken English.

And so, until school resumed in March, the camp was full of children of all ages whose mere presence and happy-go-luckiness lifted the spirits of all but the most cynical and pessimistic adults.

A simple wooden cross was the only — but constant — reminder of the camp's September tragedy, the debris of the fatal fire having been disposed of long ago.

*

The children went back to school in March at which time Cyril and the Action Committee had a problem: they could not honestly report any progress with the government negotiators who were now asking for more frequent meetings with a sense of urgency. Before long the Great Hall reports of another meeting with this or that government negotiator, a man or woman of more or less importance or influence, became predictable. But now, for the first time, as their second summer on the Point turned to their second autumn, and the protesters began preparing for another winter, the government negotiators began talking seriously about eviction.

The Committee agreed that forced eviction was sounding increasingly possible — even likely — but decided not to raise the subject in the Great Hall.

At least not yet.

The arrival of autumn dampened the protesters' mood somewhat. But the cooler weather was the least of their worries. Rather, they couldn't help being alarmed when they now saw official government negotiators being escorted to the Great Hall with one or sometimes two Peace Officers. Many or even most Kiwilanders had had unpleasant experiences with the Peace Force and were naturally unnerved by their presence in the camp. Nor could the suddenly-wary campers help but notice that the official visits were now both more frequent and longer.

At last Cyril had to warn the campers, at a meeting in the Great Hall on the evening of Easter Sunday, that negotiations with the government were breaking down. Perhaps, he had to admit, their protests and occupation were going to be futile — at least in the short term — and that eviction was possible if not probable.

'Meanwhile, carry on as normal,' was Cyril's message to the meeting.

That was his public message although he knew the government's threats were no longer empty. He thought, therefore, that they should begin making plans for an event that now seemed inevitable.

But where to start?

*

Towards the end of April, at the end of a day which had been especially cool and blustery on the Point, Cyril Flitcroft walked alone down to Beach Road and then up and across the fields of his farm, idly and automatically eye-checking the health of his placidly grazing herd, patting some on the rump as he passed through. He was looking forward to a hot bath which he needed more for its therapeutic effects on his worried mind than the cleansing of his body.

He had just climbed the stile, set into the fence which separated his mother's garden from the adjacent paddock, when he heard the croaky laughter of boys — boys on the brink of manhood — coming from the garden shed. He stood for a minute, listening to the boys — he knew Mot-L must have been in the shed with Arthur — and suddenly realised that young Arthur would be fourteen in June; he couldn't remember the date. He felt guilty, again, that he had been so busy, so selfishly preoccupied with the occupation, that he hadn't spent more time with his son.

'So he's still seeing the Vandier boy,' Cyril said to his mother in the kitchen.

'Nearly every day, after school.'

'Strange, though,' said Cyril. 'Given his father and that. What's going on?'

Ida slipped a casserole into the oven, shut the oven door, wiped her hands on her apron, turned to her son and shrugged.

'It's strange times, son,' she said. 'Strange times indeed.'

'Does he ever say anything? About the boy's father? Or what the boy says or thinks about the occupation? I mean...'

'He never says nothing,' interrupted Ida quickly. 'Not about that, anyway.'

'Strange,' said Cyril again.

After dinner, in the house, before he returned to the Point, Cyril asked Arthur, as gently as he could, whether he and Mot-L ever discussed the occupation.

'Sometimes,' said Arthur warily.

'What does he think, do you think?'

Arthur shrugged. He obviously didn't want to talk about the subject at all.

'You must...' began Cyril impatiently, but his mother interrupted him.

'Don't quiz the boy, son,' she said sharply.

'Sorry,' said Cyril.

'He said you're all going to get evicted,' Arthur blurted out, loudly and suddenly.

'What?'

'That's what he said,' said Arthur, quietly this time. He was looking down at his empty plate.

'When?'

'Just today. He said it today.'

'No,' said Cyril impatiently. 'Not that. Did he say *when* it was going to happen? The eviction?'

Arthur shook his head grimly.

21

THE ACTION COMMITTEE members now knew that eviction was inevitable, although they didn't know when or how it would happen. They assumed — were certain — that the time was near but they didn't know what to plan for because they had no idea how the government would go about physically evicting three or four hundred people; and then, having somehow forced them off the Point, what they would do with them and to them. They decided, therefore, that while they were discussing and formulating plans for the eviction they would try to act normally and encourage the campers to do the same, to follow the camp's daily routines and to continue to plan for winter.

However, despite their best intentions, nothing could stop the Action Committee's knowing and worried members from unconsciously releasing their anxiety into the camp's atmosphere where it was received by the highly sensitive antennae of worried campers who were now aware of the government's growing impatience.

Two weeks later the tension was broken — for the Action Committee in the first place — when Arthur came up to the Point after school seeking his father. He found him in the Great Hall, sitting at a table with the members of the Action Committee, including Alfred. They were looking at a whiteboard on an easel, beside which a young woman secretary from the office was standing, making a list of bulleted notes beside a diagram.

The meeting fell silent, stopped suddenly, when Arthur appeared at the table, tugging gently but silently at his father's sleeve. The standing secretary quickly moved in front of the whiteboard in an attempt to block the young intruder's view.

'Arthur. What the hell are you doing here?'

'Papa, I must talk to you,' said Arthur quietly, trying to be discreet.

'Not now, boy,' said Alfred to his grandson, trying to mitigate Cyril's brusqueness.

Arthur was suddenly aware that everyone was looking at him; he was the centre of the meeting's attention. He had clearly failed in his intention to tug gently and unnoticeably at his father's sleeve and whisper in his ear.

'I'm sorry,' he said to the meeting in general. 'But, Papa,' he stage-whispered to Cyril.

'Not now, son!' Cyril almost shouted at him. The others at the table felt and looked embarrassed.

Alfred signalled a short back-handed wave to the still open double doors at the other end of the Great Hall. 'Later, boy,' he said with uncharacteristic mildness and a sly wink.

'But, Grandpapa...'

He was interrupted by Cyril who was now angry. 'Arthur. Get out now!' he shouted.

'But...'

'Now!' shouted Cyril again. 'And shut the doors as you go.'

Arthur, hurt and embarrassed, slunk away from the small meeting, through the long and otherwise empty and almost dark building. But when he reached the open doors of the Great Hall he made a decision. He stopped, turned, and looked back to the meeting, which had not resumed; the meeters were still looking at him, waiting for him to leave.

And so he decided.

'The Peacies are going to come and throw everyone out and burn down the whole camp and everything,' he shouted, determined but afraid, before running outside, slamming the double doors behind him, and running home.

*

'They wouldn't listen,' said Arthur. He was sitting in the kitchen with his grandmother, shaking with fear and anger.

'What do mean they wouldn't listen?' asked Ida, who left what she was doing and sat at the table with her frightened grandson. 'Who wouldn't listen? Your father?'

'Yes. Papa. And Grandpapa. And all the people. They were in a big, important meeting. They wouldn't let me say anything. They just chased me away.'

'Oh my God,' said Ida.

'But I told them anyway,' said Arthur defiantly. 'I shouted it out to them and ran away.'

'And then what did they say? Did they listen then?'

'I don't know,' said Arthur. 'I told you. I ran away. I ran home.'

'Oh my God,' said Ida again.

Arthur looked pleadingly at his grandmother across the table.

'I'm really going to be in for it now, Grandmama, aren't I? Papa was so angry. About his important meeting. All those important people.'

Ida Flitcroft shook her head sadly. 'I don't think so, boy,' she said.

At which point Cyril Flitcroft stormed into the kitchen. He and Alfred had left the meeting immediately Arthur had shouted his news and run away. But while Arthur was able to run barefoot quickly all the way — down to Beach street and across and up the Flitcroft farm paddocks — his father could only walk fast, in heavy boots, while old Alfred brought up the rear.

'What the hell's going on?' asked Cyril angrily, looking directly at Arthur who, afraid, was shrinking back in his chair.

'Cyril!' shouted Ida this time. 'Leave the boy alone. Can't you see? You're frightening your son.'

Alfred came in then; he was out of breath and had to fall back into an armchair.

Cyril looked down at his father and then pointed across the table at Arthur. 'Papa?' he asked. It was a plea for help.

Alfred looked at his wife at the table and, breathing deeply, merely asked her the obvious question: 'What happened, woman? What's it all about?'

And so, as Cyril then collapsed heavily into his chair at the table, resting his elbows on the table and his head in his hands, and Arthur looked nervously at his now silent father, Ida told the two men what had happened.

'It's so simple, if you'd only listened to the boy,' she said. 'His friend, Mot-L, came here after school as usual. He's a very polite boy, as you know, and speaks to me in perfect English. So Arthur came out of his room, done his homework and everything, he said, and they went to the shed as usual.'

'So?' said Alfred. 'Get to the point, woman. About the Peacies and that. What the boy said.'

Cyril, though, said nothing. His head was still in his hands. He looked worried. Arthur, watching and listening, began to feel sorry for him.

'They'd only been gone a minute or two when Arthur rushed inside and told me.'

'Told you what, dammit?' said Cyril looking up and staring at his mother.

'That's enough of that,' said Ida angrily. 'Don't speak to your mother like that.'

'I'm sorry, Mama,' said Cyril. 'But...'

'I know,' said Ida. 'Arthur wanted to tell you himself but you've frightened the living daylights out of him.'

'Mama, please,' begged Cyril.

'Arthur here came in and told me that Mot-L told him that his father said the government was going to get the Peace Force and the Republican Army...'

'The *army?*' Cyril and his father, taken aback, exclaimed the word together.

'... and the army, that's what he said. The Peace Force and the army's going to close down the camp, the whole occupation, chuck everyone out, and bulldoze the whole lot. Burn everything.'

'That's what the Vandier boy said?'

'His father's the Superior of the whole Peace Force, son.'

'Not the *whole* Peace Force,' corrected Cyril. 'Just Northland. But that's enough. *And* the army?'

'That's what he said.'

'I tried to tell you straight away, Papa,' cried Arthur. 'But...'

'I know, son,' said Cyril. 'I'm sorry. I really am. So where's Mot-L now?'

'He went home when he told me,' said Arthur. 'He said he shouldn't have said anything but he couldn't help it. He said it's not fair.'

'Don't worry, son,' said Cyril, kindly now. 'I reckon when his father told him he knew what he'd do.'

'That's what I thought,' said Ida.

'Me too,' said Alfred. 'He's sending a signal.'

'Received and understood,' said Cyril. 'But when? Did he say anything about when, son?'

Arthur said nothing but grimaced, and shook his head slowly.

22

THE ACTION COMMITTEE was relieved to know at last that the eviction, mentioned loosely at first by the government's negotiators, in veiled threats, but more explicitly in recent meetings, was now confirmed as more than just a threat. Evidently — if Arthur's friend was to be believed, and there was no reason to doubt the germ of his message — the government was preparing to use both the Peace Force *and* the army to effect an eviction.

'And probably soon,' said Cyril.

'Using the army's a bit extreme,' said Oscar Bladen, the formerly mild-mannered undertaker who had originally been served the official government decree, taking the village's beach land, which precipitated the current occupation of the whole of Flitcroft Point. 'It's like they're expecting war.'

'Surely they won't actually *use* the army,' said Cyril. 'Just a show of force, don't you reckon? To intimidate us more.'

'Well, it *will* intimidate a lot of people,' said Oscar.

The rest of the committee nodded gloomily in agreement.

'We've got to be prepared,' said Cyril.

'Remember the lessons of history, said Beatrice Heveningham, the young history professor who had been drafted onto the Action Committee. 'Civil disobedience. Passive resistance. Non-violent confrontation.'

'It's all just talk.' The sceptic was Doreen Wombourne.

'It'll work,' said Beatrice Heveningham. 'Maybe not at once, but history shows that those tactics demoralise the enforcers and get more public support.'

'Really? asked Doreen.

'Really,' insisted the professor. 'For us to fight back would make the Peacies look like heroes. We'd look like outlaws.'

'Agreed,' said Oscar. 'And, anyway, we could never fight back and win. Not against the Peacies *and* the army.'

'We have to convince everybody that it's the right thing to do,' said Cyril. 'With non-violence we *will* win. I'm convinced.'

'That's easy for you to say, Cyril Flitcroft,' said Doreen. 'Now you just have to convince everybody else.'

'But we'll have to hurry,' said Oscar Bladen.

'We knew something was brewing,' said Cyril to a full meeting in the Great Hall. 'It started after Easter when the government wanted more and more meetings. Each time they said they had a better offer. But each new offer, while better than the last, was still ridiculous.

'And don't forget,' he emphasized, 'they're trying to sell us land that's been ours all the time. We know it. And *they* know it.'

There was a murmuring of discontent from the audience.

'The thing is,' continued Cyril, 'they were playing for time. They thought we'd have given up by now, what with winter on the way and that, but we haven't.

'And we *won't!*'

Such oration from Cyril — or anyone — always brought clapping and cheering. It did so on this night too. But it was a somewhat subdued response, arising more from habit than fervour. It suggested that the campers were impatient; that they'd heard it all before.

Cyril correctly sensed then that all the protesters really wanted to hear about was the eviction and what the Action Committee planned to do about it.

'But now the government seems to have lost patience,' he continued. 'Now, it seems certain, they're going to come up here with the Peacies and even the army to evict us all...'

At this point Cyril's words were drowned out by boos and protests louder and longer than the half-hearted applause which had followed his opening remarks.

At last. That was the feeling of the meeting; a feeling shared by every one of the protesting campers. Now, at last, they knew the protest was reaching a climax.

*

Cyril couldn't sleep.

He had to believe what Arthur had told him. New information.

'He said it will be on Monday.'

That was on Friday afternoon, following Arthur's usual after-school meeting with Mot-L.

'They've got the whole weekend to prepare,' Cyril had said, more to himself than to Arthur. Then, to Arthur, he said, 'Thanks, son.'

'But, Papa, what are you going to do?'

'They've got the whole weekend to prepare,' he said again. 'And so have we.'

Now it was Sunday night. The weekend was over. They'd done everything they could. Everyone was prepared. Tomorrow was the big day.

But Cyril couldn't sleep.

He checked the time: ten past two. In the morning.

So, he thought, Arthur's Monday, which is what the Vandier boy told him after school, is now today.

Today. But when? The boy didn't say. Just Monday. Today.

The thought made sleep impossible. He took a blanket, went out into the dark and cold and walked barefoot through the quiet, sleeping camp, down to the end, to the point, where he sat on the bench which the builders had put there so that the daytime view — and *what* a view it was — could be admired in comfort.

The night-time view was different. A black sky pulsing with countless billions of stars around a thin moon. The sea was barely moving although he could hear the soft fall and gurgle of small waves on the rocks below the point.

It was a fine but cold night towards the end of May, not quite three weeks since Arthur had finally conveyed the inevitability of the eviction. He wrapped himself in the blanket and sat down. His feet were cold. He should have put on shoes but it was too late now.

Atilla, one of the patrol dogs, emerged silently from a nearby bush and lay down at his cold feet. He could feel the dog's warmth. He gently manoeuvred his icy feet until they rested under the dog's hard but warm and furry chest. Atilla turned and looked up at him as if to show that he understood and didn't mind.

Cyril smiled to himself.

Murray Ambrose, Atilla's owner, who was in the middle of his night patrol shift, arrived and sat down on the bench beside Cyril. He looked up.

'Nice night,' he said.

Cyril nodded.

'Big day tomorrow,' said Murray, looking out to sea.

Cyril looked at Murray and nodded again with a nervous smile. 'Today now,' he said.

'S'pose so,' said Murray. 'Probably my last night doing this.'

'Probably,' agreed Cyril.

'Well, everyone's ready, Mr Flitcroft,' said Murray. 'Don't worry about that. Everyone's ready.'

'Good on you, Murray,' said Cyril.

They both looked out to sea while Atilla looked up at Murray, anxious to get moving.

'Better get on, eh,' said Murray after a silent while. 'Come on, boy.'

Atilla stood up and Cyril again felt the cold air around his feet and ankles.

'See you, Murray,' he said.

'Tomorrow, eh,' said Murray.

Cyril nodded.

Today, he thought. Hard to believe that it'll soon all be over. After, what? More than five hundred days, they reckon. Five hundred and six days. Something like that. And then what? What will happen? Will we ever get Flitcroft Point and the beach land back? What if we don't? And can't help thinking of poor Doral Turpin. What a waste.

God, I'm tired.

What a couple of years, he thought. Starting with poor darling Fannie. Fannie and the baby. The fact is — he had to admit it — I probably wouldn't have done any of this if her and the baby had lived. The farm. And Arthur. Mama's been good. A mother for Arthur. But her and Papa are getting on. Both, what? sixty-seven, nearly sixty-eight. And poor old Enoch. What a life he had. Anyway, after Fannie and the baby, it freed me up, I suppose, that they died like that. Just then. Just when the government decided to walk all over us again.

So now what? After all this time. Planning the occupation. The Action Committee. The meetings in the Great Hall. Organizing support from all over the country. Keeping spirits up, especially last winter. All the futile meetings with the government agents and negotiators. The meetings with the Kiwiland Labour Council. Probably couldn't have done much without their support.

And now, tomorrow. Today. Soon. But when?

I wonder what'll happen. Arthur should be all right. And his friend? Well, they'll never find out about him, I'm sure about that. But me, the committee, Papa, all the rest of us. Hundreds of us. What will they do to us?

I suppose we'll just have to wait and see.

23

'BLOODY HELL, THEY'VE even sent the navy.'

Alfred Flitcroft was standing with Cyril and the rest of the Action Committee, looking down the Flitcroft Point sloping path to the Beach Street gates, waiting for the arrival of the expected eviction party — however it might be constituted — when he turned and noticed a heavily-armed cruiser of the Republican Navy rounding the headland to the south. It looked to be heading for a position off Flitcroft Point.

And then, just as Cyril and his companions had turned their attention seaward, in response to Alfred's astonishing observation, a loud shout came from the young watchman in the lookout tower.

'Here they come! I can see them!'

They, too, saw them then. The Action Committee. And everyone else. All the tense and nervous protesters who had received their final briefing the night before, Sunday night. Standing. Waiting. Watching. Silently. They all saw them coming.

It was nearly ten o'clock on the morning of Monday the twenty-fifth of May.

Given the time, Cyril realized that they must have assembled and prepared in Whangārei — just as Arthur's informant had said — before travelling to the coast.

The green-uniformed Peace Officers came first. A long and ragged double file of them. A hundred or more, Cyril guessed. Perhaps two hundred. They were walking, rather than marching, from the village and down Beach Street. And then, as the head of the Peace Force lines reached the camp gates — now open and unguarded — and the tail came over the hill from the village, they were followed by the camouflaged soldiers of the Republican Army, three abreast, marching with military precision.

'They're not armed,' said Oscar Bladen with relief.

'But they've got the navy aiming their guns up here,' said a frightened Doreen Wombourne.

'Just for show,' said Beatrice Heveningham, the only other woman on the Action Committee.

'Just for bloody show, the bastards,' said Alfred.

'God, I hope everyone remembers what we've been talking about all week,' said a worried Cyril.

He said it to his father but he didn't take his eyes off the advancing Peace Officers. They were now coming up the slope, rather casually he thought, and spreading out to form a long line which eventually encircled the whole camp, presumably to foil any escape.

'It'll be all right, boy,' said his father nervously.

I hope so, thought Cyril as he quickly mentally went over the preparations which they had finalized at the camp's last meeting the previous night in the Great Hall.

All the women and children had been sent home except those two women on the Action Committee and a few others, old and young, without children to care for, who insisted on staying.

'Now don't be embarrassed,' said Cyril to all who remained. 'Be honest with yourselves. Feel free to leave tonight if you don't want to be arrested. For any reason. Go now. You won't be judged. Tomorrow won't be fun. Not everyone's cup of tea.'

Then, before the camp was closed for the night, everyone had been instructed to take home absolutely anything of value — sentimental or monetary — as well as clothes and bedding, anything not needed, and especially food. Meanwhile, the office staff had already taken all the computers, servers, records and files of any and every sort to be stored in the village's Great Hall on the Flitcroft farm.

'We don't how this is going to pan out or when we'll be back, and the camp won't be guarded,' Cyril warned the meeting. 'We can't afford to leave our stuff lying around for the government or looters or anyone else.'

There was no argument from the floor.

Finally, before closing the camp for the night, they went over, again and again, what they would do — or rather wouldn't do — if they were to be physically ejected from the site. That part of the meeting was again, and for the last time, led by the young history professor, Beatrice Heveningham, who had become a vital and respected member of the Action Committee.

'Please, tomorrow, remember everything we have been through,' she had insisted.

She was a charismatic speaker. Everyone listened and believed her every word, phrase, sentence and sentiment even though they'd heard them all before.

'If you are approached and spoken to,' she said, 'say nothing. They could try to threaten you, or intimidate you, in which case just ignore them. Look over their shoulder, or to the side, or at something interesting in the distance. Or say something trivial to your neighbour. It's a nice day today, or something like that. If you are told — ordered — to leave, stay. Sit down on the ground or just stay where you are. Don't budge. If you are handled physically it's important that you don't react physically. Don't resist. Don't push or shove the Peacie or soldier away. Don't say or do anything provocative that could be misconstrued. Basically, don't say or do anything at all. If they start to pull you, push you or otherwise force you to move, just go limp. Collapse in a heap. Make them drag you away.

'If we fight back we'll look weak not strong. If there's violence from us we'll lose all the support we've gained since the beginning,' she continued forcefully. 'But when the Peacies start to move us, dragging and carrying us, especially when they start manhandling the old men and women amongst us, then it'll be them, and the government for that matter, who will lose support. No one — Kiwilanders or Vandiers — will enjoy watching that sort of spectacle.'

'There'll be about three hundred of us, we think,' said Cyril, 'so if they really want to physically evict us off the site it'll take them ages.'

And now, as Cyril and the others watched, Professor Heveningham's words became facts.

The Peace Officers began to tighten the circle. And, although they were outnumbered, each officer seemed to randomly select someone to intimidate, preferably someone smaller than he.

Without saying or doing anything, each officer went up to his selected target and stood face to face, uncomfortably close, closer than any person ever puts his face to another's unless they are lovers. The protesters, without exception, while naturally unnerved, didn't move or flinch.

Cyril was confronted — although, in his case, at a civilized distance — by the Superior of the Peace Force, Mot-L's father, whose name Cyril suddenly realized he didn't know. Nor did he know whether the man wondered how and why the whole camp was ready and waiting for the arrival of his men.

He suspected that he did.

Exactly what words passed between the two men, each equally staunch in his role in the confrontation, is not known. But it was clear to observers that, whatever they were, they were exchanged, in Vandient, with courtesy and mutual respect.

It was, of course, a conversation which had to be had; a mere formality. Each man knew, in advance and without doubt, what the other would say and that the outcome was inevitable.

The official demand having been given, received, and rejected, the Superior of the Peace Force stepped back, nodded to his second-in-charge, and so the process began.

Each of the protesters being confronted by a Peace Officer was asked to leave Flitcroft Point.

When they refused to respond in any way, let alone leave, they were arrested.

They were then forced to line up, a few at a time, their images numbered and captured automatically. They were carried or dragged away, the arresting officer recruiting the help of a colleague, down the slope of the Point where they were bundled, one at a time, into one of the army transporters which had followed the soldiers and were now waiting on Beach Street.

Until then the army had played no role in the eviction. Now a few soldiers were engaged in running the transporters back to Whangārei and guarding their passengers during the journey. The rest, many hundreds, were stood easy on the lower slopes as a few pieces of the army's heavy machinery, including a mechanical digger, three small bulldozers and a few trucks, arrived on the scene.

Cyril was, of course, one of the first to be arrested and removed. Thus he was not witness to the complete eviction. But as he left, as he was dragged with his father and others down to the waiting transporters, he noticed with sadness that many of the soldiers were Kiwilanders.

He knew there were some Kiwilanders in the Peace Force — a few — but he had forgotten just how much the army depended on Kiwilander recruits who, he knew, were attracted by the promise of steady employment and a regular wage, free accommodation for his family, higher education for himself and his children, trade training, and, not least, the camaraderie of a disciplined organization with shared values and goals.

Above all he knew that the army's recruitment policy was necessarily blind to differences of race, religion, culture and language; thus it promised its soldiers and officers a level of security not easily available to Kiwilander civilians having to live in a Vandier world.

It was, he knew, sad but true.

24

IT TOOK THE Peace Officers all that morning and most of the afternoon to complete the arrests. Many of those arrested had to wait, sitting at the edge of Beach Street beside the camp fence, guarded by the soldiers, while the army transporters returned from Whangārei. In all, two hundred and twenty-two protesters were formally arrested. Many Vandier supporters were amongst them and the irony of Kiwilander Peace Officers arresting Vandier protesters was not lost on anyone on either side.

Processing began at the Whangārei courthouse as soon as the first of the army transporters arrived, which meant that Cyril, his father, and the rest of the Action Committee, were amongst the first to find themselves in the courthouse cells.

By the time all those arrested were in Whangārei it was clear that the courts would have to work late into the night to complete the processing.

Eventually, during a break late in the evening — taken so the magistrates, court staff, attending Peace Officers, soldiers and the prisoners themselves could be fed — the Superior of the Peace Force was officially informed that the courts were overwhelmed by the number of arrests. Indeed, by that time, so late in the evening, only thirty of the protesters had been processed. Furthermore, he was told, first-processing protocols alone would take several days, especially as many of the prisoners insisted on defending themselves in English; translators would have to be found and that would not be easy.

And anyway, said the chief magistrate by way of admonishment, the Peace Force should have known that there were not enough facilities and accommodation to hold and feed so many prisoners for so many days, and nor was there enough staff to supervise them.

The Superior of the Peace Force and his senior colleagues were therefore persuaded to return all the arrested protesters to the village without delay, including the thirty men and women processed but awaiting their hearings. They were assured that all two hundred and twenty-two of them would be recalled to court, in due course and order, and in manageable numbers, to be processed and sentenced.

However, insisted the chief magistrate, the protesters were to be informed that it was a condition of their temporary release that they could not — *must* not — return to the Flitcroft Point site and their encampment there.

The army did not itself return the protesters to the village. Rather, it chartered a special V-3 Local service to the village from the Whangārei V station so they would be returned, together, in one journey. Thus it was late, dark and cold before the protesters arrived at the village. Most — hungry, tired and emotionally wrought — went straight home with relief.

Alfred, too, went directly home to Ida.

'Bloody hell, woman,' he said, 'I'm bloody exhausted.'

'You're too old for all this nonsense now, Alfred Flitcroft,' said Ida sympathetically.

'I think you're right.'

'So, what happened? Tell me all about it.'

'I need a hot bath,' said Alfred. 'Then I'll tell you.'

'Where's Cyril? Isn't he with you?'

'He's gone down to have a look.'

'There's burning,' said Ida. 'You can see it out the back. Flames and smoke and everything.'

'I saw it from the station. And Main Street.'

'It looks awful,' said Ida. 'I think they're burning everything.'

'Probably are,' said Alfred gloomily. 'Where's the boy?'

'He's down there too,' said Ida 'Watching the fires. Been there since he got home from school.'

*

Arthur wasn't watching the fires any more. He was in the cemetery, sitting at the foot of his great-grandfather's grave, looking out at the blackness of the sea. His mother's grave was on his right, his friend Doral Turpin's on his left.

There was a sickle moon but it was more often than not hidden behind the thin, wintry clouds of late May. And, anyway, its light was cold and ineffective.

He could still see the flames from the three bonfires burning on Flitcroft Point, high and to his left. Sometimes, randomly, the flames reached and writhed high above the burning piles, as if trying to escape to the sky, and were reflected briefly in the black sea. And there was stinking smoke. It was being blown away by the same chill wind that was moving the wispy clouds.

He was thinking then about the four dead people in whose company he sat. Of his mother and little unborn brother, dead now for two whole years. He thought — through his sadness — how strange it was that his mother knew nothing about the occupation of Flitcroft Point which had so dominated his own life, his father's, his grandfather's, and old Enoch's while he lived. And it was at the foot of his mother's grave, on his right, that he first met Mot-L, the clever and curious young Vandier who so wanted to learn English and lately played such an important role — evidently sanctioned if not encouraged by his father — in the drama of the eviction of the Flitcroft Point occupation.

He remembered ancient Enoch at whose feet he was now sitting. He thought of the old man's great age and the memories and certain knowledge he carried around in his head which had given the protesters confidence that history couldn't be denied, was on their side, and that, this time, at last, justice would prevail. Now, though, seeing the fires and the ruins of the occupation, it looked to Arthur as if old Enoch was wrong. He was glad that his great-grandfather had died before discovering how wrong he could be.

And then, finally, Arthur remembered his friend, Doral, lying on his left in the cold earth, and he didn't know what to think. So he thought nothing.

*

Meanwhile Cyril had walked down Beach Street from the V station. He saw the glow of the fires as soon as he turned off Main Street and knew immediately what had happened in the hours since his arrest.

The gates were closed when he reached them, guarded by unsmiling and unresponsive soldiers of the Republican Army. He looked up the path and saw that the Great Hall had collapsed and was now no more than the biggest of three bonfires. He could see it had been fed with the remains of the camp's sheds, huts, tents, rugs and carpets, and other kitchen and office equipment, all of which had evidently been pushed into the fire by a bulldozer now parked to one side. A few soldiers were engaged in collecting scraps of wood and other material missed by the bulldozers and tossing them almost playfully into the flames.

Two other smaller fires blazed, one higher up the Point, the other closer to the coast, each with its own resting bulldozer and attendant soldiers.

Cyril stayed for an hour or so before wandering home, depressed, despondent and utterly pessimistic. It was then he learned that Arthur was still out.

'He went down there after school,' said Ida. 'I thought you'd find him down there.'

'There were a few people still there,' said Cyril. 'I never saw him.'

Arthur had fallen asleep across old Enoch's grave. He was found there by Cyril, cold and miserable, who had guessed where he'd be, although he'd expected him to be at his mother's grave, not Enoch's.

'Is it all over, Papa?' asked the boy sleepily as they trudged up Beach Street together.

'Looks like it,' said Cyril.

'Did we win?'

Cyril shook his head slowly.

'I don't think so, son,' he said. 'I don't think so.'

The official records show that after two months of legal debate by the magistrates of the Whangārei courts the Flitcroft Point dispute was referred to the Department of Justice in Auckland. The Whangārei magistrates had learned that many of the country's leading and most respected law firms were preparing to vigorously defend every case brought against the two hundred and twenty-two arrested protesters, one at a time, which they feared would clog up the courts for many months or even years.

That was, said the magistrates, utterly untenable.

As a result, after due consideration by the justice committee of the Supreme Court, given the legal history of both the disputed site and the adjoining strip of beachside land — history already known to the learned members of the justice committee as well as the country's leading jurists, historians and academics — it was decided that the government's case against the defendants was probably indefensible which meant that, in the committee's view, none of the proposed prosecutions would succeed. It was recommended, therefore, that proceedings against all the protesters be dropped and that sentences already pronounced be revoked.

Furthermore, the committee recommended that the government should halt all proposed development of the Flitcroft Point land until both sides had presented their arguments to an independent tribunal whose decision would be final and binding.

Epilogue

IT IS NOW the end of 2178 when the story of the occupation of Flitcroft Point must end.

The independent tribunal is still sitting. It is too soon to predict what might happen. However, there are hopeful signs that as the government is forced to hear the evidence and legal arguments put to the tribunal by the Kiwilanders' lawyers it is becoming uncomfortably aware of the many actions and inactions of governments, past and present, which were plainly unjust. It is possible that a new conscience, even a mild sense of guilt, is arising in government ranks which could, perhaps, lead to some form of compensation for the Kiwilanders.

But even if all the land stolen or acquired cheaply or by deceit or force from the native Kiwilanders of the past is eventually returned to the Kiwilanders of the present, or fully paid for, as a result of conscience, guilt or simple human decency, will it be enough?

After more than a hundred years of cultural denigration, land dispossession and consequent privation, has the spirit of the Kiwilander race been broken beyond repair?

Is it too late?

Only time will tell.

— THE END —